D1622942

CRITICAL
VULNERABILITY

ALSO BY MELISSA F. MILLER

An *Aroostine Higgins* Novel

CRITICAL VULNERABILITY

MELISSA F. MILLER

THOMAS & MERCER

Published by Thomas & Mercer, Seattle

www.apub.com

Amazon, the Amazon logo, and Thomas & Mercer are trademarks of Amazon.com, Inc., or its affiliates.

ISBN-13: 9781477849415
ISBN-10: 1477849416

Cover design by Megan Haggerty

Library of Congress Control Number: 2014952000

Printed in the United States of America

CHAPTER ONE

Thursday afternoon

Sidney Slater was ordinarily not a yeller. At worst, he treated the assistant US attorneys who worked beneath him in the Department of Justice's Criminal Division with mild disdain and poorly hidden contempt, as if he were so much smarter than his underlings that he couldn't really fault them for any perceived failings. But today he seemed to be making an exception especially for Aroostine.

His face was a mottled purple, and spittle actually sprayed from his lips as he shouted at her.

She wondered idly if he might have a stroke.

"Are you listening to me, Higgins?"

Unless he had a soundproof door, everyone in the office was listening to him. She decided to keep that point to herself.

"Yes, sir."

"This was supposed to be a slam dunk. The company already settled; all you had to do was prosecute the individuals. You *begged* me for a shot. Said you were ready to first chair a federal case. Didn't you *assure* me you wouldn't screw up this trial? Didn't you?"

Slater half-rose from his desk chair and slammed his palm down on a stack of papers, sending them fluttering across the carpet.

She bent to retrieve them, taking her time and letting her long hair fall across her face like a black curtain. Only when she was certain she had rearranged her expression to mask her own rising anger did she straighten to standing and hand him the papers. She had sacrificed too much for this shot—so much that she couldn't bear to think about losing it.

"Yes. I did say that. And I am ready. I'm not going to screw up, Sid."

She hoped her neutral tone would inspire him to calm down, but it seemed to have the opposite effect. His eyes bulged out, and his voice grew louder.

"I don't care! Don't waste time pointing your finger at someone else. Tell me what the devil you plan to do about this motion *in limine*."

She tilted her head and tried to figure out why he was so worked up. The fact that the defendants' lawyers had filed a motion to exclude evidence wasn't exactly unheard of—it was fairly standard. Yes, the particular piece of evidence that they wanted to keep out of court was critical to her ability to prove her case, but she didn't think their argument was even all that persuasive. What was she missing?

The motion asked the judge to prohibit her from introducing a crucial two-minute-long tape-recorded cell phone call between the two individual defendants—sales representatives employed by the software company that had settled. During the call, they detailed their efforts to bribe a Mexican government official.

For obvious reasons, the defendants didn't want the jury to hear them, in their own words, admit to clear violations of the Foreign Corrupt Practices Act. And it was likely true that without the recording, the government wouldn't be able to convict the salesmen. But Sid's reaction was extreme—did he expect her to have somehow prevented the defendants from filing the motion?

He was staring at her stony-eyed. Waiting for her to say something.

"What do I plan to do about it?" she finally asked, buying time.

"Yes, Higgins," he said through clenched teeth. "What do you plan to do?"

"Well," she said carefully, "I was thinking I'd oppose the motion." She bit back the rest of what she wanted to say—*You know, like every other lawyer in America would do in response to totally ordinary motions practice?*

"You don't know, do you?" The anger seemed to leak out of him all at once, leaving nothing but resignation.

"Know what?"

"Your opposition is due today."

She shook her head at him. "That can't be right. The case management order said oppositions to motions *in limine* are due eight days before the trial. I have, what, a month and a couple days? In fact, I don't know why they filed it so early."

Sid sighed and shuffled through the papers on his desk.

"I don't know why you didn't get this. Judge Hernandez issued an order on Monday moving up the trial date. Jury selection starts a week from tomorrow."

What?

He pushed the paper into her hand, and she scanned the order numbly, ignoring the blood rushing in her ears.

"How can he do that?"

"He's the judge. He can do whatever he wants."

"But *why* would he?"

"Because as the most liberal appointee on the bench, Judge Hernandez seems to think it's his solemn duty to yank my chain whenever he can. That's probably why he had this so-called courtesy copy sent over."

DC politics. Of course.

"I still don't understand why I didn't get an electronic notification, though." She scrolled back through her memory. She was *sure* she hadn't missed an e-mail from the court system.

Sid rubbed his forehead. "The court system just switched over to a new database. They did the work last weekend, so none of the active cases would be impacted. But, apparently, as usual, they screwed up."

Adrenaline washed over her, and she tried to keep her voice steady. "I can't get an opposition drafted that fast. I'll have to ask for an extension—"

"You will not."

She blinked.

He went on. "You'll find a way to get it done. There's no way the Department of Justice is going to go begging for more time."

She considered pointing out that he was cutting off *her* nose to spite his face, but she didn't have time to waste arguing with him. She had fewer than ten hours to research, draft, and file an opposition to a motion *in limine* that would tank her case if it were granted.

"Understood. I'll get something on file, no problem. You won't regret giving me this case, Sid."

He shook his head in disgust and waved her to the door. "I already regret it. Just get it done."

Aroostine yawned. Her back was tight, her neck was stiff, and her eyes burned. The wave of nervous energy that she'd ridden through the first several hours of the evening had waned and finally evaporated. She was drained. She rolled her shoulders, then rubbed her eyes with her fists and checked the time.

11:30 p.m. No wonder. Way past her bedtime.

Even when she'd been in law school, during exams, she'd kept to her schedule while her classmates were chugging Red Bull and pulling all-nighters.

Joe used to call her Ben Franklin because of her early-to-bed, early-to-rise habits.

He had a point: her natural rhythms were closely tied to sunrise and sunset. She rose at dawn and did her reading before breakfast. After classes or work, she would study hard with no breaks, not even one, straight through from dinner until nine o'clock. But then, as the old clock on the mantle chimed the hour, she capped her high-lighter, powered down her laptop, and drew a hot bath. She'd be in bed, lights out and, at least according to Joe, snoring adorably by nine thirty. No exceptions.

Joe.

Unbidden, a picture of Joe, his mouth curved into a gentle grin and a teasing glint in his clear blue eyes, popped into her fatigued mind. The memory made her chest ache. She closed her eyes and blinked away his image and, with it, the tears she didn't have time to shed. She couldn't afford to be distracted by thoughts of Joe.

She had to maintain her focus. The motion was nearly finished. All she had left to do was confirm all her case citations were correct, then upload the document to the court's electronic filing system. She ran the program to cite-check the cases and waited for it to spit out its results.

She scanned the results and, satisfied, e-signed the opposition and loaded it to the court's site. A wave of accomplishment and relief washed over her. She'd met the deadline with a few minutes to spare.

She started to pack up so she could drag her tired body home. But now that the work deadline had passed, Joe resurfaced in her mind. She felt her frustration and rage building.

Before she realized what she was doing, she picked up the smooth, heart-shaped stone she used as a paperweight and whaled it at the wall. It hit the cloth-covered particleboard with a satisfying thud and fell to the institutional carpet.

She wasn't ordinarily a thrower, but *man, that felt good.*

Until about twenty seconds later, when she heard light tapping at her door, and her office neighbor eased it open to peer inside.

"Everything okay in here? I heard a noise." Mitchell examined her from behind his tortoiseshell glasses.

She felt her cheeks flush.

"Uh, yeah, I . . . dropped my paperweight." She gestured lamely toward the gray heart on the floor.

"Dropped it, huh?"

"Dropped it."

He tilted his head and fixed her with a curious, but not unkind, look.

She stared back at him, defiant, daring him to call her out.

Instead, he stooped to pick up the stone. "Here you go," he said, dropping it into her open palm and giving her a crooked smile.

"Thanks." Her fist closed around the cool rock.

"You look tired. Are you trying to make a midnight filing deadline?"

"Not anymore—I just filed it. You, too?"

She checked her watch. If so, he'd better hurry. He had one minute.

"Even worse. Writing a white paper."

She scrunched up her face in empathy.

As she was learning firsthand, there was plenty of grunt work involved in being an assistant United States attorney. But writing white papers that set forth the government's positions on various legal matters was quite possibly the most thankless of all the mundane tasks performed by the cadre of AUSAs who served in the Department of Justice.

For one thing, the position papers had to be perfect, beyond reproach by any legal scholar or desperate litigant. For another, they weren't bylined, so the authors received exactly no credit for writing them. And, finally, they weren't optional. Everyone was expected to pitch in and produce a white paper when called upon to do so.

And in Sid's division, no reason was good enough to beg off— not being in the middle of a trial, out on maternity leave, or simply devoid of even a scrap of familiarity about the topic. When Sid said it was your turn, you dropped what you were doing and wrote a white paper. Simple as that.

"Ugh," she said in solidarity.

"You can say that again. I've had back-to-back depositions all week. And, of course, this thing is due by the end of the day tomorrow. I've just gotta crank it out." He smiled ruefully at his bad luck.

She tried not to notice that he had a very warm smile. Some people might even call it sexy.

"Well . . . good luck," she said in an obvious and awkward attempt to get him to return to his drudgery so she could pack up and go home for some much-needed sleep.

Mitchell either couldn't take a hint, or he chose to ignore the one she lobbed his way.

"You know, actually, it's nearly midnight. I'm pretty sure I've reached the point of diminishing returns. Let's grab a drink and kvetch about our lot in life in nicer surroundings? I know a really good wine bar near Chinatown."

Her spine stiffened. Her palms grew damp. She forced herself to meet his eyes.

"Thanks, but I'll have to pass. I don't drink."

He just grinned.

"Do you eat?"

CHAPTER TWO

Three days earlier

Franklin Chang came home from work at the usual time and let himself in through the front door. He stamped the fine dusting of snow off his shoes and dropped his briefcase to the floor. It was only Monday, but he was already bone-tired. He'd spent his entire weekend switching over the federal district court's computer database to a new system and then the whole day dealing with irate court clerks because some underling had failed to check the box to turn on electronic notifications.

He opened his mouth to yell to his mother to let her know both that he was home and that she'd left the door unlocked again. She didn't seem to grasp the fact that he had literally hundreds of thousands of dollars' worth of the latest technology crammed into the little starter home. He loved the neighborhood, which was why he hadn't moved someplace posh outside the Beltway, but he didn't intend to bankroll the local juvenile delinquents with a steady supply of easily pawned equipment.

The words never came. He gaped at the picture frame hanging at a wild tilt in the foyer, the overturned side table, the smashed lamp.

He tripped over the briefcase and ran toward the back of the house. He raced through the ranch house, room by room. His tiny, tidy house had been ransacked, but nothing was missing. Except his mother.

A trail of blood stained the tile in the hall bathroom. It led from the bathroom, down the narrow hallway, through the kitchen, and out the back door. It stopped at the edge of the alley—right where a person might park a car if they didn't want to be seen from the street.

He dismissed the thought and tried to convince himself that she'd fallen and had summoned help. But that possibility rang hollow even to him. If she'd been injured, he'd have been the first person she called. And even if, for some reason, she'd called a friend or a neighbor instead, someone would have gotten in touch with him. He checked his phone with trembling fingers: no messages, no missed calls.

After he stopped shaking, he walked back through the house, out the front door, and began to canvas door-to-door. No one in the quiet, close-in neighborhood had seen either his mother or anything out of the ordinary. Hyattsville, Maryland, wasn't one of those crime-ridden areas where people kept to themselves and closed their eyes to the violence around them, either. His neighbors were always outside, doing yard work, walking their dogs, or generally getting into one another's business. The local kids played stickball in the street and sat on the curb to eat empanadas from the Salvadoran place down the road. Someone should have seen *something*.

But it was as if she'd vanished into thin air.

As the minutes ticked into hours, his anxiety skyrocketed, and he found himself nibbling on the skin near his thumb. He sat out on the porch, shivering in the cold night air, as if his presence outside would somehow make his mother return.

An arc of headlights washed over him, as the woman who lived directly across the street drove by him and turned into her driveway.

She emerged from the car and began gathering armloads of groceries from the trunk. Seeing Mrs. Johnson jolted him to action.

He chewed off the flap of flesh and crossed the street, very aware of his stinging skin as he walked.

After helping her carry the bags into her house, he stood there awkwardly while she thanked him and tried to shoo him back out the door.

Finally, he kicked at her scuffed linoleum and cleared his throat. "Uh, is Tyrone home?"

She jerked a thumb toward the den, where the television blared, and shouted, "Tyrone, Mr. Chang from across the way wants a word."

She turned back to Franklin. "I'm gonna get out of this work uniform. He'll be right with you." She eyed the bags on the counter, waiting to be unloaded. "You want anything?"

"No, thanks." He smiled in what he hoped was a casual way.

She examined his face for a long moment and then headed up the stairs. As the sound of her footsteps faded, Patrolman Tyrone Johnson emerged from the den. He cut a massive, hulking figure, even in a plain white t-shirt and his uniform pants.

"You want one?" Tyrone raised a beer can in Franklin's direction.

"Um . . . no thanks. Listen, I'm sorry to bother you. I just need some help."

Tyrone's relaxed face hardened into an unreadable expression. "What'd you do?"

"Nothing! I swear—my mom's missing."

"Missing how? Like, she's late getting back from her book club or something?"

"Missing like there's blood all over my house and no trace of her. As far as I know, her book club doesn't meet this week. Neither does her card club or her knitting club. She should have been home watching her *Downton Abbey* videos. The whole season's due back at the library tomorrow." He realized he was babbling but seemed unable to stop the words that were tumbling out of his mouth.

"Doubtin' who?"

"Never mind. It doesn't matter. Should I file a report?"

Tyrone painted him with an exasperated look. "Don't you watch TV, man? She's an adult. Until she's gone for twenty-four hours, we can't do shit. Come on," he said, shrugging into a plaid flannel shirt.

"Where are we going?"

"The police can't do anything, but you can. We're going to check the local hospitals, clinics, and bars."

"Bars?"

"Your ma's no spring chicken. You'd be surprised how many of these old folks have an episode and wander off and you find them sitting on a barstool, talking the bartender's ear off."

"My mom has a glass of sherry at the holidays. Maybe some wine out at a restaurant. That's it."

"Whatever." He laced up his boots, then turned and bellowed up the stairs, "Gloria, I'm goin' out for a bit with Franklin. You see his ma, call my cell. You hear?"

Above, a bedroom door creaked open. "Hear? The whole street heard you, you fool." The door banged shut.

Franklin spent the next hour on an awkward scavenger hunt with his taciturn neighbor. He was glad for the company, even though their search proved futile. Somehow, Tyrone's massive, silent presence settled Franklin's nerves.

Tyrone dropped him off with instructions to call the station the next day and ask for the missing person's desk. Franklin stood on the porch and watched him cross the street back to his house.

"Mom?" he called as he walked inside. A blanket of silence greeted him. His panic came rushing back in a wave, and he paced around the living room.

Where was she? Was she hurt?

Franklin's cell phone vibrated to life in his pocket. He checked the display. *Unknown caller.*

"Hello? Mom? Where are you?"

An unfamiliar voice said, "No. This isn't your mother, Franklin. Listen very carefully. Go to your mailbox and remove the gift I left you. Turn it on."

"Who is this?" he demanded to an empty line. The caller had already hung up.

Feeling numb, Franklin walked out onto his porch. Inside the metal mailbox, he found a cheap flip phone—the kind of prepaid phone that bodegas all over the city sold to illegal immigrants who couldn't contract for service with any of the major carriers.

He stepped back inside, then powered it on. It began to ring immediately, and he nearly dropped it in surprise.

"H-h-hello?" he stammered, unable to keep the nerves out of his voice.

"I have your mother. She is unharmed. For now."

"You have her? Who is this?"

"That is not your concern."

"Wait, you're lying. You hurt her. There's blood all over my house."

A put-upon sigh sounded in his ear. "An unfortunate accident. She panicked and fell. She hit her chin on the corner of the sink. This cut, it bled copiously, but it was a superficial wound. You may ask her yourself."

There was a pause and a muffled noise, then Franklin heard his mother's voice.

"Franklin, is that you?"

"Mom, yes, it's me! Are you okay?"

His mother answered in a careful voice. "I'm fine, honey. I don't know what this gentleman wants you do to, but he says if you do as you're told, he'll bring me home." He heard the tears she tried to choke back. "Please do what he says."

"I love you, Mom. I'll find you," he managed before the man's voice came back on the line.

"You will not find her," the man assured him. "You will never see her alive again unless you follow my instructions to the letter. I will be in touch when I need you."

CHAPTER THREE

Franklin punched ten memorized digits into the prepaid cell phone with shaking fingers, then wiped his sweaty hands on the thighs of his khakis. While the call connected, he swallowed several times in a futile attempt to wet his very dry mouth.

On the second ring, the man answered.

"Is it done?" he asked without preamble.

"Yes."

"You are sure?"

"I'm sure," Franklin said. "She filed the motion at two minutes to midnight. Exactly at midnight, I deleted it. The opposition motion is gone from the system, removed without a trace."

He picked at his ragged cuticles and waited.

Finally, the man intoned in his stilted English, "That is good."

Franklin wondered, not for the first time, about the hint of an indeterminate accent. And decided, not for the first time, that he probably really didn't want to know where the man was from. The less he knew, the better. Or so he imagined.

"Um, so, I held up my end of the bargain . . ."

"Yes."

Franklin waited for a moment, but the man didn't seem to pick up the hint.

"So, we're good? You'll let her go?"

The man barked out a dark laugh. "No."

Anger collided with fear in Franklin's gut. "We had a deal."

"The deal has changed. I will be in touch with further instructions."

"Further instructions? No, I can't—"

"You can, and you will. Unless you wish for me to kill your mother. Is that your desire?"

"What? No!" Franklin yelled the word as his heart squeezed in his chest. He forced himself to keep breathing.

"This is good. Goodbye."

"Wait—no, don't hang up. I want to talk to her. Please?" he added hastily.

Silence.

He could hear the man's slow, even breathing as he considered Franklin's request.

"She is unharmed."

"So you say. But I need to confirm that for myself. You haven't let me talk to her since Monday. How do I know she's even . . . alive?" Franklin grimaced at having to say the words, but they were true.

"You do not trust me?"

"You just reneged on our deal! Why should I trust you?" Franklin blurted. Then he bit down on his lip so hard he tasted blood. "I'm sorry. I didn't mean that. I just—please. Please let me talk to her?"

The man huffed. "She is sleeping. If the lawyer asks for a delay or offers a deal, I will release her. But, until then, until the trial is no longer a threat, I need you. And as long as I need you, your mother stays where she is."

"But I saw the docket. The trial isn't scheduled to start until the Monday after next. That's ten more days. Can't you please let her go? I promise, I'll do whatever you want."

"No." The man's voice was firm. "However, when I call you with your next assignment, you may speak to her."

Franklin was gearing up to demand, plead, cry—whatever it took to convince his mother's captor to let him talk to her. But the line went dead with a sharp click before he could marshal his argument. He stared at the silent phone in his hand for a long moment.

Then he gently placed it on the table and ran for the bathroom as his dinner tickled the back of his throat. He was going to puke. Again.

As he raced for the john, the man's words echoed in his brain: *Next assignment. Next assignment.* What else was the man going to make him do?

Hot tears streamed down his cheeks as he crouched in front of the bowl and heaved into it.

CHAPTER FOUR

The wee hours of Friday morning

"I knew from the time I was in high school that someday I would stand up in court and say 'Mitchell Swope, on behalf of the United States of America.'" He smiled sheepishly and stared down at his scrambled eggs. "Corny, huh? I guess I watched too much *Law & Order*."

She kept her face blank, but she thought his idealism was endearing. Cute, even.

"It's not corny at all," she assured him, cupping her hands around the mug of hot chocolate to warm them.

The walk to the all-night diner had been short, but a cutting winter wind had chilled her straight through. Rich, piping hot cocoa seemed like the obvious solution. But then she'd had to find a menu item that worked with the hot chocolate. So, while Mitchell devoured a hearty breakfast, she was savoring a thick slice of apple crumb pie. Whipped cream and all. She told herself she'd run an extra mile tomorrow, knowing it was a lie.

"What about you? How'd you end up at Justice?" He settled back against the cracked faux leather booth and pinned his eyes on her with a look of genuine interest.

"My path was less straightforward than yours. I majored in English in college and did my senior thesis on *To Kill a Mockingbird*. When I met with my career counselor to discuss job options after graduation, I kept picturing myself as Atticus Finch, practicing law in a small town. So, I went on to law school and worked summers for a solo practitioner. He taught me what I needed to know to run my own practice. I set up shop in my hometown as soon as I passed the bar exam. Who sounds corny now?" She laughed at herself.

He shook his head. "Not corny at all. Lots of people land in law school because they have dreams of six-figure salaries or they don't know what else to do with a political science degree. You had a vision and the nerve to go out on your own as a baby lawyer. But how'd you get from there to here?"

She cut off another bite of pie with the side of her fork and said, "I'd been practicing all of about six months when I got a call from the Pennsylvania Supreme Court. I don't know if you heard about this scandal, but about a year and a half ago, a judge was murdered in Springport. It was all over money, of course. A dirty council-woman and her sister were working a bunch of different angles to profit from the hydrofracking boom."

"Yeah, sure. And the state attorney general was involved, too, right?"

"Yes. So the Commonwealth was looking for an outsider to serve as special prosecutor to look into the AG's role in the whole mess. The solo lawyer I had worked for had a weekly tee time with two of the justices on the Pennsylvania Supreme Court. He suggested me and told them I was squeaky clean. I guess the idea of a twenty-first century Atticus Finch wannabe had some appeal to them."

"You were, what, twenty-six years old and a special prosecutor?"

"Twenty-five. So, after that case, my private practice really picked up and I had settled into a nice groove, but then the prepper thing happened—"

"The prepper thing?"

She sipped her hot chocolate and wondered how much she could say. The prepper thing hadn't been quite as well publicized as the dirty state attorney general thing, even though it had been a much bigger deal. Homeland Security kept a tight lid on the fact that, just a year ago, the country had been teetering on the edge of a global pandemic that could have wiped out most of the population and the entire infrastructure.

"It's a really long story. But the short version is there was a big, multi-agency federal investigation in Clear Brook County, the same place where the judge was killed. And the team needed some local help—"

"Let me guess. Your retired solo practitioner plays cards with the Director of Homeland Security?"

She giggled. "Close. There's this big shot white-collar criminal defense attorney in Pittsburgh. A guy named Volmer. He represented one of the witnesses in the grand jury investigation—another lawyer by the name of Sasha McCandless. You follow?"

"So far. I feel like I need a cheat sheet. This is like one of those Russian novels with a million characters."

She raised an eyebrow. "Russian literature fan?"

"Guilty as charged. Anyway, go on."

"So Sasha was appointed to investigate the death of Judge Paulson back in 2011, and she testified during my investigation. Then last year, she got herself caught up in this other mess with the preppers. *Her* boyfriend—well, husband, now—is former Homeland Security. When the prepper investigation heated up, his old boss asked him for the name of a local attorney who could help them navigate the small-town culture. They had this enormous team of big-city lawyers getting doors slammed in their faces all over town. Nobody wanted anything to do with them. Will and Sasha remembered me and passed my name along."

"What did you do exactly?"

"Mainly, I just made introductions and convinced people to cooperate. These people knew me, and they trusted me. I guess the team liked me, because when the opening came up in the Criminal Division, Sid called me up."

"*He* called *you*? You just fell into this job?"

She shrugged. "I guess you could say that."

His fork clattered to the Formica table.

"That doesn't happen. People angle for our jobs for *years*. Internships, clerkships, miserable stints at big law firms. You just walked in from your small-town practice because you were local counsel on a Homeland Security case? *And* you're first chairing the SystemSource trial?"

Her stomach knotted at the reminder. "Yeah."

He whistled. "Nice. What kind of case is it?"

"SystemSource settled an FCPA charge stemming from efforts to bribe a Mexican government official to buy their industrial control system. Even though the company settled, the two former salespeople who handled the Latin American territory and actually attempted to bribe the guy insist on going to trial."

"Is your case solid?"

"It is now. I was filing my opposition to their motion *in limine*. Assuming Judge Hernandez doesn't do something crazy, I have the evidence to nail these guys to the wall."

He groaned. "Not Hernandez."

"Why?"

"Hernandez *hates* Sid. I mean, really hates him. Our win percentage in front of that guy is abysmal. Your case isn't quite the plum assignment I thought it was."

Her chest turned to lead, but she ignored her dismay. "Well, the judge can hate Sid all he wants, but the jury will see the case for what it is," she insisted.

A shadow passed over his face.

She knew he was thinking of all the ways a motivated federal judge could shade a case to change the jury's mind.

But he didn't challenge her bravado directly.

"I hope so."

She checked her watch and gasped.

"What?"

"It's one thirty."

"Do you turn into a pumpkin?"

"Something like that. I'll be dead on my feet tomorrow. I have to get home."

He must have heard the panic in her voice, because he didn't try to argue with her. He looked around, caught their worn-out waitress's eye, and gestured for the check.

"Go grab a cab. I'll take care of this."

"I can't let you pay for me, but I'd love to take off if you don't mind waiting for the bill."

She pressed ten dollars into his palm and gathered up her belongings. She wound her scarf tightly around her neck and steeled herself against the chill she knew would hit her when she walked out the door.

CHAPTER FIVE

Friday morning

Aroostine groaned as the winter sun beamed through her slatted blinds and hit her square in the face. She opened one eye to squint at the alarm clock on the bedside table, then rolled over and buried her head in her pillows.

Her tired body was stiff. And her brain was stuffed with cotton. But it was already seven thirty.

Ten more minutes, she told herself and slipped back into her dream.

A sleek beaver sat on a boulder under a low harvest moon. The moonlight glinted off its glossy coat. The animal watched her watching it for a moment, then shifted its gaze to the stream rushing by below, cold water glistening in the night. Aroostine followed its gaze. Down the hillside, across the water, and up on the opposing hill, set among the tall trees was a small log cabin. One yellow square of light shone through the sole window facing them.

The beaver turned its silver eyes back to her. She could sense the animal trying to communicate something important about the little house.

Then the harsh beeping back-up alarm of a garbage truck in the alley behind her building penetrated her sleep.

Friday morning. Trash day.

She forced her eyes open and rolled over. Soon clatters, clangs, idling trucks, and shouted instructions from one orange-coveralled worker to another would fill the air as the row of Dumpsters that lined the back walls of the buildings on her block were emptied.

Whatever that beaver was trying to tell her would have to wait for another night. She pushed off the warm, heavy handmade quilt that she'd burrowed under and stood. Her toes curled in protest as they hit the cold, bare wood floor.

As she raced across the floor to the bathroom, she told herself she'd stop at World Market and pick up a colorful rug this weekend. Even as she thought it, she knew it was a lie. She'd been making that same empty promise every week for sixteen weeks. But she never bought a rug—or any other home goods, for that matter. She was still holding out hope that one evening she'd come home from work and find Joe on her doorstep, along with the cheerful braided rug that anchored their bed, Rufus on his long, retractable leash, and a box full of lamps, bookends, and the assorted small touches that had made their house *home*.

She turned on the water full blast and stepped into the shower, thoughts of Joe filling her mind. As the hot water pelted her head and neck from the fancy rainforest showerhead, she let her tears flow freely.

It's not going to happen.

For reasons he hadn't shared with her, Joe had decided not to join her in DC, even though he said he would. He just never showed up. His silence fed her fantasies that, any day now, he'd come be with her, but how long could she go on kidding herself?

You need to move on.

She reached for her shampoo bottle, and Mitchell's face swam into her mind.

She blinked water out of her eyes and shook the image out of her head.

The last thing she needed was to develop a crush. Let alone a crush on a colleague.

She had a massive criminal trial to prosecute. Jury selection started in one week. If she didn't focus, she might as well start boxing up her meager belongings and get ready to crawl back to Central Pennsylvania with her proverbial tail tucked firmly between her legs.

The thought of admitting defeat to Joe set her teeth on edge and drove thoughts of romance—with anyone—straight from her mind.

Like hell she would.

She finished showering quickly and rushed through her morning routine, keeping one eye on the time as she dressed. She reheated a bowl of baked oatmeal and wolfed it down while standing over the sink. Then she gathered her papers, pulled on her coat, and raced out the door.

She jogged the three long blocks to the Metro station, dodging the commuters who kept a more leisurely pace. She was usually sitting behind her desk, well into her workday and her second mug of cinnamon tea by the time the DC morning rush heated up.

Not today. She had to jam her way through the turnstile and stand shoulder-to-shoulder on a packed Metro, swaying at one with an overheated sea of humanity.

By the time she'd pushed her way through the crowd and raced up the steep staircase to the street, she was hot and frazzled. Just how she wanted to start her day.

At least it's Friday, she consoled herself as she zigzagged around a tour group and into the perfectly ordinary F Street high-rise office building that housed the Criminal Division.

She flashed her badge at the security guard stationed in the lobby and trotted to catch the elevator that a trench-coated arm was holding open for her.

"Thanks," she said to man as the doors closed.

"Sure thing."

She squeezed herself into a corner of the car, jostling up against suit-jacketed shoulders on both sides.

When she'd interviewed for the job, she'd met with officials at the Pennsylvania Avenue headquarters, which was exactly as she'd imagined it: an imposing, impressive limestone building that took up an entire block of the National Mall, complete with columns and carved sculptures on the facade and a detailed mosaic on the entryway ceiling. Everywhere she'd looked she'd seen polished bronze and aged marble. The awe she'd felt had played a good-sized part in her decision to accept the position.

Only, as it turned out, Aroostine didn't work in the Robert F. Kennedy Department of Justice Building. She worked a little more than half a mile to the northwest and a world away from the grandeur and the power of the headquarters building. The Criminal Division leased plain vanilla office space in a regular old office building that served to inspire no one.

The elevator groaned to a stop on her floor, and she eased her way out from the pack of office workers, turning sideways and pulling her elbows in close to her body to prevent knocking a to-go cup of coffee out of a clutching hand and setting off a caffeine-fueled riot.

As she walked down the long hallway, she fished her identification badge from her pocket by its lanyard. She flashed it at the card reader, waited for the *click* to signal that the door had unlocked, and then pushed it open.

She made it all of ten feet inside before she was ambushed.

"Did you get an extension, after all?" Rosie Montoya called, poking her head out of the kitchenette tucked behind the reception area.

"How did you even know it was me?"

The hallway wasn't visible from the kitchenette.

Rosie emerged from the space with a mug of muddy coffee in one hand and a container of yogurt in the other.

"They came in early today and installed these cool digital displays in the common areas—there's one in the library and one in the big conference room, too. When someone swipes a card, his or her name pops up on the readout. It's gonna make stalking the boss so much easier," Rosie said, grinning.

Not just the boss; the rest of us, too, Aroostine thought.

She said, "I'm surprised there's not one in the bathroom. There's not one in the bathroom, is there?"

The junior lawyer laughed. "Not yet. Give them time. So?"

"So?"

"Did you get an extension or what?"

"No, I filed last night—with two whole minutes to spare."

Rosie wrinkled her forehead. "That's so weird."

"What?"

"It's not showing up on the docket."

Aroostine felt her own brow furrow. "It has to be."

"It's not."

Electronic filing was instantaneous. The opposition appeared on the docket within a minute, maybe less.

"That's not right. I got the confirmation from the system last night." She'd double-checked it before she'd left with Mitchell.

Rosie looked at her blankly and shook her head. "It's not there. I've refreshed the docket a half-dozen times this morning."

"Come with me." Aroostine headed down the hallway, trailed by the junior attorney. They reached her office door and she snuck a quick peek at Mitchell's door, but it was closed.

She wasn't sure if the feeling that swept over her was relief or disappointment. Either way, she didn't have time to analyze it.

She powered on her laptop and waited for Outlook to open. She leaned over the desk and scrolled through the unopened e-mail messages that had hit her in-box since midnight until she found the automated confirmation message.

"See?"

She opened the message and clicked on the hyperlink in the body of the e-mail, which would take her directly to the filed version of the opposition.

Only it didn't.

She stared at the 404 error message that filled the screen.

"That's impossible."

She clicked over to the docket to try to reach the file that way and blinked. The last entry on the docket was the court's order rescheduling the trial. The entry before that was the defendants' motion *in limine*.

Where was the opposition?

Her palms grew damp, and her mouth went dry.

"I don't . . . Where'd it go? I filed it. I got the confirmation."

Rosie peered over her shoulder at the monitor. "It must be a glitch. I wouldn't worry about it. You did get the confirmation."

Her words were reassuring, but Aroostine could tell the younger lawyer was as baffled as she was.

"*Mierda*," Rosie swore, pointing a manicured nail at the blinking e-mail icon. "The judge just entered another order."

Aroostine hurriedly clicked the notification, and her heart dropped into her stomach as she read the text of the short order.

Defendants' Motion in Limine to Preclude Recording (Doc. #42) is granted as unopposed.

"Oh my God. I'm going to puke."

Rosie pushed her into her desk chair.

"Listen, don't stress about this. I'll get on the phone with the clerk of court. I'm sure it's just some kind of weird mistake. We'll get it cleared up, and Judge Hernandez will issue a new order."

Aroostine searched Rosie's eyes. As always, it struck her that looking at Rosie was like looking in a mirror. Despite their disparate ethnic backgrounds, Rosie's Hispanic features and her own

Native American characteristics were almost identical. They shared the same coloring, the same glossy black hair, the same brown eyes, and the same bone structure. Add to that the fact that they were both within an inch or two of six feet tall, and it was no surprise that people constantly asked if they were sisters.

Right now, Rosie's pale, tense face belied her casual confidence and probably mirrored her own expression. Aroostine really did feel like she might vomit.

"Hernandez hates Sid," she mumbled. "What if he doesn't issue a new order?"

"He will."

Aroostine closed her eyes and focused on her breathing until the wave of nausea passed.

"I hope you're right."

"I am; you'll see. Let me go get this straightened out."

"Thanks, Rosie."

"No worries." She started out of the office and then turned back. "Oh, I totally forgot. I heard an interesting piece of gossip this morning."

"Yeah?" Aroostine feigned interest.

"Rumor has it Sid's on the short list for a promotion."

"Good for him."

"It's good for you, too, you know. If he gets the bump, Tony Henderson is a lock to take over his job. And you know what that means?"

"We'll all have to pretend to be Redskins fans?"

Rosie ignored the jab at Henderson's football mania. "His job will be open."

"And?"

"And if we can pull off a guilty verdict, you'll be the logical candidate to replace him as deputy."

"In what universe?"

"The one where you win a big FCPA case and happen to be a coveted double minority. That universe."

Aroostine winced.

She didn't consider herself any sort of minority. For one thing, roughly half the world was female. And for another, she'd been adopted by a prosperous white family when she was seven. The Higginses had given her everything she needed to build a foundation: stability, love, shelter, clothes, education, and support. She wasn't disadvantaged, and she hardly needed a leg up. The federal government's insistence on giving her extra credit for the accident of her birth was a constant irritant. Like dust in her eye.

"Hey, are we running today at lunch?"

Rosie blinked at the subject change, and, despite herself, Aroostine swallowed a laugh.

Her discomfort must have been more extreme than even she realized. She *never* suggested running. Usually, Rosie had to threaten to drag her bodily from her desk chair or bribe her with cupcakes to get her to lace up her running shoes.

"Uh . . ."

"You know, exercise gets the brain moving, too. And if we're going to win this trial, a little extra brainpower will come in handy."

"Okay, sure." Rosie gave her a look like she'd grown an extra head, but she went along with the idea. She left the room, pulling the door closed gently behind her.

Aroostine tried to put the docket mishap out of her mind and started working through her endless to-do list.

CHAPTER SIX

Franklin chewed on the cuticle around his left thumb without realizing it. The raw skin bled easily, and he looked down in surprise when he tasted blood.

Disgusting, he thought. On top of everything else, now he had a gross nervous habit, thanks to the man.

The thought of the nameless man made Franklin's heart pound with impotent anger. He'd promised that if Franklin tapped into the federal court's docket system and made a stupid document disappear, he would return Franklin's mother unharmed. If Franklin didn't—or if he contacted the authorities—he said he would give Franklin directions as to where he could find her corpse.

And Franklin had done everything exactly as the man wanted. The man, whoever he was, clearly knew enough about Franklin's work to realize that deleting a record from the electronic docket would be child's play for Franklin.

Although he'd never before done anything more illegal than fail to come to a full stop at a stop sign, he had access to an array of systems and networks that most hackers couldn't imagine in their most power-hungry dreams.

He was SystemSource, Inc.'s lead programmer. That meant he was in charge of testing and debugging the company's flagship off-the-shelf industrial control systems product, RemoteControl. SystemSource sold the RemoteControl system to office buildings, residential apartment buildings, government agencies, hospitals, colleges, private companies—anybody who wanted to control and monitor complex systems remotely. Which was just about everybody. Why pay a guard to sit in your building and watch your surveillance cameras, when you could outsource that task to some guy sitting in his living room monitoring your cameras, controlling the HVAC systems, making sure the elevators stopped on all the floors, and keeping pretty much every essential system running?

To enable the company to provide real-time support, updates, and monitoring to its customers, Franklin left a door open in the configuration data of each unit. He was the only person at System-Source who knew how to get into the configuration data, and once he was inside, he could gain access to the administrator's password and, from there, the username and password of any user. Logged in as an employee, he could control whatever systems that login identification managed.

So, when the man told him to delete the opposition to the motion *in limine*, all he had to do was log in to the electronic court filing system as the system administrator and type in the docket number the man had given him. It took him all of eight seconds to wipe away any trace of the filing.

He'd been surprised to see that the caption named his very own company as a defendant, *The United States v. SystemSource, Inc., et al.* After he'd removed the opposition papers filed by the Department of Justice, he poked around the docketed documents long enough to learn that his employer had settled with the government months ago, paying a thirty-million-dollar fine but not admitting wrongdoing.

The only defendants still remaining were two former sales representatives, Craig Womback and Martin Sheely—men he'd never heard of, let alone met. The two had overseen the company's fledgling Latin American division and were charged with bribing Mexican government officials.

He thought that would be the end of it, but of course the man had reneged. And now he spent his working hours looking over his shoulder, worried that someone inside the company was involved in his mother's abduction. Who else would know that he could access the docket?

This new worry made him even jumpier and more paranoid—a state he didn't even know was possible.

As if to prove the point, the cell phone rang, and he leaped, nearly spilling his French roast on his wrinkled khakis.

"Jeez, buddy, switch to decaf," one of the interns said as he strolled by Franklin's cubicle.

Franklin ignored the guy and hissed into the phone, "Hello?"

"Your employer was awarded the contract to install a new security system at the Criminal Division's F Street location. Are you aware of that, Franklin?"

"Yes," Franklin said, his stomach sinking. The system had just come on line a few hours earlier, and he'd spend the first part of the morning testing it to ensure it was working properly.

"Of course you are," the cold, foreign voice continued. "What you may not know is that your company won that contract over a year ago. The start date and installation were pushed back until SystemSource settled the FCPA lawsuit. It would have been very embarrassing if your American taxpayers learned that the Department of Justice was business partners with one of its criminal defendants, no?"

Franklin was distracted by the man's use of *your* in front of *employer* and *American*. Was it a slip of the tongue or did he not care that Franklin knew he wasn't connected with SystemSource and wasn't a US citizen? Or had he said it because he *was* a System-Source employee and he was trying to throw Franklin off his track? God, the last thing he needed was for this terrible man to think he was on his track.

"No?" he prompted.

"Oh, yes. I'm sorry, I thought that was a rhetorical question," Franklin hurried to explain.

"Stop thinking. Answer the questions I ask and do what I tell you. Do you understand?"

"Yes, I understand. I'm sorry." He tried hard to convey his contrition to the madman on the phone.

"Good. Now, before we get to your next assignment, I believe I said you could speak to your mother. You have thirty seconds."

There was a crackle in his ear as the man must have activated his device's speakerphone feature.

Franklin wet his lips, cupped his hand around the phone, and croaked, "Mom?"

"Franklin." His mother's voice echoed hollowly through the speakerphone.

"Is he feeding you? Has he hurt you?"

"He wants me to tell you he's treating me appropriately."

"Is he, though?"

She paused. "It's not the Ritz, but I'm fine."

He thought she sounded weaker and wearier than she had four nights ago, but she'd never cop to discomfort.

Tears stung Franklin's eyes, and he gripped the phone so hard he was surprised it didn't break in his hand. "I'm going to get you home, I promise."

"He wants the phone back. I love you, honey."

His mother's voice faded, replaced by the harsh, ugly tones of her captor. "How touching."

Anger flared in Franklin's belly, but he choked it back and said nothing.

"Are you ready?"

"Yes," Franklin said neutrally.

"Good. You are to monitor the attorney who filed the opposition. The Higgins woman."

"What do you mean by *monitor*?"

The man huffed. "I mean to keep an open channel. I want you to keep track of when she arrives at work. When she leaves. Her incoming and outgoing phone calls. How long they are, who she speaks to, and what she says. When she logs onto her computer and what she does. What databases does she access? What websites does she visit? What documents does she create? What does she save? Print? Delete?"

"You—you want me to spy on her all day?"

"Precisely."

Franklin's mind raced. How was he supposed to do that all day long without anyone else in the company noticing? It simply wasn't possible.

"I don't think I have access to all that information," he lied.

"You disappoint me," the man said quietly.

There was a rustling noise, then Franklin heard a distant shrieking.

The hated voice filled his ear again. "Shall I break your mother's wrist then? To motivate you?"

Franklin's stomach roiled, and acid rose in his throat. "No, I'm sorry! Don't hurt her—I'll do it."

"Next time, there will be no negotiation, Franklin. Do not ever lie to me."

"I won't. I won't . . . Just, please, don't hurt her," Franklin panted.

"Very well. Do you understand your assignment?"

"Yes. Do you really want to know *everything* she does?"

"Everything," the man confirmed. "I will call you for regular reports. If, however, you see or hear something that you think will be of great interest to me and will hasten your mother's return, then you may call this number."

"Wait! Wait—what's of interest to you? I really don't understand."

"Be creative, Franklin. Anything that provides leverage over Aroostine Higgins."

The line went dead.

Leverage, Franklin repeated to himself silently.

CHAPTER SEVEN

Friday afternoon

Joe stroked the silky fur of the mournful golden retriever sitting at his feet.

"You miss her too, don't you, boy?"

Rufus cocked his head and gave Joe a look that said that was a stupid question.

He sighed. Of course Rufus missed her. After all, she was the one who had found him, caked with mud and shivering in a cardboard box by the side of the road. She was his mistress—the one who'd taken him in, cleaned him up, and gone on long walks with him in the woods. As far as Rufus was concerned, Joe was just some guy who was handy with a can opener.

Feeling increasingly stupid, he continued his one-sided conversation with the dog.

"She'll be back. You'll see. She just needs to get this big city lawyer thing out of her system."

Rufus whimpered, and Joe scratched his long, soft ears.

"You'd hate it in DC. Living in a cramped shoebox apartment. No backyard. No ducks to chase. No ponds to swim in. Dirty, crowded, noisy. Fast, impersonal, expensive."

Rufus nosed his hand, turned in two circles, then immediately fell asleep.

Must be nice to be a dog, Joe thought, jealous of the canine's uncomplicated emotional life.

He stared sightlessly into the dying fire for a long time. She'd been gone for four months. Maybe it was time to face the fact that Aroostine wasn't coming back.

You could go there, he told himself. She'd asked him repeatedly to give it a try. He waffled, thinking of how much he'd like to see her liquid brown eyes and hear her throaty laugh. What harm could one visit do?

No. He knew himself. He had no intention of uprooting his life and following her to DC. Even if Rufus wouldn't feel penned in by city life, *he* would. And she was working all the time, anyway. A visit would confuse things and send the wrong message.

What message is that? That you love her and miss her and you're willing to support her dreams—the way you told her you would?

Joe shook his head to get rid of the nagging, judgmental voice that sounded in his ears. His eyes fell on the papers from the lawyer's office. He knew he needed to stop delaying the inevitable and deal with them, but right now, he couldn't bear the thought.

He picked up the phone from the nearby end table and punched in the area code for Washington, DC. Then he jabbed his finger down to disconnect the call. He bounced the heavy, old cordless phone in the palm of his hand and thought.

It's Frugal Friday, he realized. Ten-cent wings, fifty-cent drafts, and bad karaoke to country music at the Hole in the Wall would chase the ghosts away.

He turned on the phone and dialed again, punching in the numbers quickly before he weakened and called her.

Three rings.

"Brent, man, you up for some beer and wings?"

"You know it, my brother."

Joe exhaled, and relief at having narrowly avoided a pitiful show of weakness flowed over him like water or, better yet, a frosty glass of Yuengling.

"Meet you there in twenty."

Rufus lifted one eyelid and eyed him disapprovingly. Then he pawed his nose, snorted, and went back to sleep.

CHAPTER EIGHT

Saturday morning

Aroostine crouched alongside the creek and listened. Most of the trees were winter-bare, and their dried, fallen leaves blanketed the ground, covering twigs and rocks.

There. A faint *crunch* sounded from the other side of the water.

She scanned the opposite bank, her eyes narrowed and focusing hard, her head cocked. Another *crunch*, this one barely audible.

It, whatever it was, was moving to the south.

She slipped through the icy water, making no sound, causing no telltale splashes. As she stalked the animal through Rock Creek Park, she felt just a bit silly. Her behavior was ridiculously out of place for an urban park. But she had to do something to clear her mind and re-center after her disastrous workweek.

Some people golfed. Others meditated or practiced yoga. Her adoptive mother knitted intricate, colorful sweaters and scarves and hats. Rosie, in an obvious display of mental imbalance, trained for and ran marathons. And Aroostine sat. She sat for hours in all sorts of weather in whatever wilderness environment she could reach and observed and tracked the wildlife. She was beginning to adjust to doing it in an urban park setting. She filtered out distant traffic noises and learned to disregard the occasional dog walkers or couples looking for privacy who ventured deep into the woods.

It was worth it. The natural world was a balm to her heart. Peace. Oneness. A connection with the planet and all its beings.

Joe had once observed that her tracking was the only piece of her heritage she'd taken along with her when she'd left her native culture behind. And as much as that statement had riled her, it was true.

She'd learned to track at her grandfather's elbow. From the time she could waddle behind him on unsteady toddler feet, she'd found refuge in the woods. It was quiet. It was calm. And he taught her that if she paid close attention, the woods would share all the secrets of the wild with her.

She allowed herself a faint smile as she stepped carefully out of the creek and bent to examine the disturbed mud and gravel on the bank.

The distinctive tracks gave the animal away. Raccoon. It had probably come to the water to wash its food and had slunk away into the woods when it spotted her.

You can't avoid the case forever, she admonished herself.

But she needed this, she reasoned. She felt increasingly disconnected from nature the longer she lived in the dense, noisy city. One morning spent mucking around in the woods wasn't going to tank the trial. Rosie's contact in the Clerk's Office would track down their wayward motion. The defendants' own words would convict them. And maybe, just maybe, the quiet stillness of the winter woods would help her rid her mind of distractions, like Joe.

She settled back on her haunches. The thin rays of sun fell on her upturned face. She closed her eyes, filled her lungs with the cold, fresh air, and emptied her mind.

CHAPTER NINE

"Do you understand?" the man asked in a cold voice.

Franklin's fear and worry masked his irritation at constantly being treated like an idiot. If this man thought Franklin was so stupid, why had he chosen him?

"I understand."

"Good. It needs to start in her home office. That's the second room on the left side of the hallway as you walk away from the door."

Franklin placed a finger on the square labeled "study" on her apartment's floor plan.

"I see it."

"Can you overload the circuit her computer is on, start a small electrical fire?"

Of course he could.

As Franklin was learning, as long as he didn't care about societal rules and the law, he had the technical ability to do almost anything. The knowledge of how much power he possessed as long as he had a keyboard was nearly as frightening as the fact that the man on the other end of the phone held his mother's life in his hands.

"Yes."

"If possible, the damage should be confined to her apartment. If it is not possible, that is acceptable. What is the goal?"

"The goal is to destroy her computer."

"Yes, very good. And you will override the sprinkler system."

"I will—to her apartment only."

"Very good. Do it."

The man hung up.

Franklin pushed away the thought of what might happen if the lawyer was sleeping in and was overcome by smoke. He couldn't get distracted worrying about other people. He had to do whatever was necessary to get his mom back safely.

He tapped into the system that controlled the Delano Towers apartment building's electrical systems and pulled up the detailed grid. He clicked on 609. A detailed plan of the apartment, with a blinking square to indicate every outlet currently being fed juice, filled his screen.

He found the study on the map and enlarged it. There was no doubt which outlet powered her computer. The bar graph at the bottom of the screen showed the overwhelming majority of the electricity going to an outlet on the north wall. Franklin assumed a lawyer would be careful enough to purchase and use a decent surge protector.

He scratched his chin. How the surge protector would work depended on whether she had one with a built-in fuse, a gas discharge arrestor, or a metal oxide varistor. Metal oxide varistors were by far the most common type. He'd just start there. A varistor worked by diverting excess voltage away from its protected load. But, by design, it worked best when it conducted electricity during a short spike or a transient surge. Exposure to a persistent overload, for as short a time as several seconds, should overwhelm it, overheat it, and cause it to burst into flames, even if she spent the money for an internal circuit breaker. He'd try that first and readjust if it failed.

He pulsed power to the line, ramping up the load to 208 volts. Then he waited. He did not have long to wait.

After about fifteen seconds, the building's sprinkler system and hard-wired fire alarms began to light up. He minimized the electrical system window. With three clicks, he overrode the fire alarm and disconnected the system that would activate the sprinkler in the study of apartment 609.

Her computer would literally melt. And the flames would take care of any papers sitting on or near the desk. The man would be pleased.

He gnawed at a flap of jagged skin hanging near his thumb.

"Please don't let her try to be a hero," he whispered aloud. The thought that the lawyer or one of her neighbors might rush into the burning apartment to save her work ate at him.

He'd be responsible for anyone who was injured—or worse.

Panicky tears filled his eyes.

His mother had always worried that he was too soft to survive in the modern world. Maybe she was right. Maybe he was so soft and weak that he would fail to save her.

Pull yourself together.

He forced himself to slow his shallow breathing and punched in the man's telephone number to let him know that he'd done it. He'd added arson to his growing list of crimes.

The sense of tranquility that Aroostine had spent an entire morning cultivating evaporated in an instant when she rounded the corner onto her street and saw the crowd of residents huddling on the sidewalk and in the street near her apartment building. A small fire truck blocked the street, and parka-wearing police officers directed the mass of people to stay back.

Aroostine spotted Mr. Cornhardt, who lived across the hall in 610, standing with the Indian couple from the end of the floor. He wasn't wearing a coat but had a knitted afghan thrown over his shoulders. Peanut, his Westie, was whimpering in his arms. She noticed that, unlike his owner, Peanut was bundled into a jacket.

"What happened?" she asked as she approached the group.

The Indian woman's eyes widened when she saw Aroostine.

"Oh, Aroostine. There's been a fire," Mr. Cornhardt said, his voice trembling. At the sound, Peanut started to shake.

"There, there, Peeny," he soothed the dog.

"A fire? Was anyone hurt?"

"No, thank the Lord. But Mrs. Patel here says one of the building managers told her it started on our floor."

"In your unit actually," Mrs. Patel said in a soft, apologetic voice.

"My apartment caught fire?"

Aroostine's mind reeled. Where would she stay? How bad was the damage? Were her belongings all destroyed?

"You have renter's insurance, don't you?" the Indian man—presumably, Mr. Patel—asked.

"Yes," she said numbly, trying to claw through the shock to remember her agent's name.

"That's good. We heard it was an electrical fire. It started in the walls."

"But . . . I have a surge protector," she said.

Mr. Cornhardt shook his head. "It wasn't a surge. Nobody else noticed anything out of the ordinary. I was watching *Ocean's Twelve* with Peanut here. He likes that George Clooney. *Ocean's Eleven* is a clearly superior movie, but the second one was free with my streaming account, and Peanut isn't very picky. Anyway, my power never flickered or anything."

The Patels nodded their agreement.

"But, how . . ."

"I don't know. You need to find someone from building management and get some answers. They're crawling all over the place in a panic because your sprinkler malfunctioned."

Aroostine just stared at him wordlessly.

"It's true," Mr. Patel chimed in, "the fire alarm didn't go off and neither did the sprinkler."

"Are those . . . connected?" She didn't think they would be, but she hadn't ever had a reason to think about it. At the moment, her brain was struggling to make sense of the jumble of words her neighbors were throwing at her. Engineering details were definitely beyond her grasp.

"Two different systems," Mr. Cornhardt confirmed. "And they've tested them both. They're both working properly now, including in your unit. So, why are we still freezing our butts off in the street? That's the real question."

Mrs. Patel gave Aroostine a sympathetic smile. "You must have very bad luck. If they let us back in, you'll join Ajit and me for dinner tonight."

"That's very kind of you, Mrs. Patel."

"Call me Dia."

Aroostine forced her mouth into an approximation of a smile.

"Thank you, Dia, but I'm afraid I have a case getting ready to go to trial, and I really need to work this evening. Can I get a rain check?"

"Certainly," Ajit said.

"Thanks. Well, at least I finally met my neighbors," she joked.

Over Mr. Cornhardt's shoulder, she spotted Mallory, one of the building managers, talking to a burly man wearing a Fire Department windbreaker. She excused herself and jogged over to them.

You must have very bad luck.

The matter-of-fact statement echoed in her head.

First her missing document. And now this. It was certainly beginning to seem that if it weren't for bad luck, she'd have no luck at all.

She approached Mallory and the firefighter and cleared her throat.

"Oh, Ms. Higgins," Mallory squeaked when she noticed Aroostine standing there, "I'm so sorry to have to tell you this—"

Aroostine took pity on her and finished the sentence, "My apartment caught on fire. I talked to the Patels and Mr. Cornhardt."

Mallory released the tension she'd been holding in her shoulders. "Obviously, the Delano will replace anything that's been damaged or destroyed by the fire or smoke."

"Great." Aroostine smiled weakly. "So, what exactly happened, and, more important, when can I get into my apartment?"

"You 609?" the firefighter interrupted.

"I guess so. My friends call me Aroostine, though." She surprised herself with the lame attempt at a joke.

It earned her a reluctant chuckle. "Well, Aroostine, an electrical fire started in the wall, which blew your surge protector, melting your computer and destroying pretty much everything in your home office as a result of a malfunctioning sprinkler." He threw Mallory a dark, disapproving look at the mention of the sprinkler failure.

"Melted my computer?" Aroostine repeated stupidly. "Like, my hard drive?"

"Afraid so."

For the first time since her neighbors had broken the news, the enormity of what had happened hit her.

"Aroostine? Are you okay?" Mallory asked, a look of concern on her face.

"I . . . just . . . I have a trial starting in a little over a week. All my notes . . ."

"Surely you back up to the cloud? Or keep a copy at the office?" the firefighter said in disbelief.

"Usually, both. But not these notes."

"Why not?" Mallory asked, her concern morphing into judgment.

Aroostine closed her eyes and willed herself not to pass out. She swallowed and said, "It's a long story. It doesn't matter."

She wasn't about to tell the property manager and some random District of Columbia fireman that she was so insecure about her trial abilities that she didn't want anyone else to stumble across her opening, closing, and witness examinations and cross-exams until they were final.

Pride goeth before the fall, her adoptive father's voice rang in her ears.

She almost laughed. She'd never truly understood that particular adage until this very moment. Fat lot of good it did her now.

"Anyway," she pressed. "Can I get into my place?"

Mallory and the firefighter exchanged a look.

"I'm sorry, but no," he said.

"Look—what's your name, anyway?"

"Pete Richards, ma'am."

"Look, Mr. Richards, I've been out in the woods all morning, and I need to take a shower, change my clothes, and get something to eat before I go into work. Because *apparently* I need to recreate my trial prep notes from scratch. So, can you please stop being a bureaucrat and let me into my apartment?"

"No can do. Your walls are still hot. And it's smoky in there. It wouldn't be safe." His voice was kind, but his face was implacable.

Aroostine felt tears welling up in her eyes and forced them back. "What am I supposed to do?"

Mallory hurried to reassure her. "We can put you up in the model apartment temporarily. And I'm sure I can get the office to approve a petty cash dispersal so you can get some clothes and toiletries. It'll just be for a night or two. Luckily the damage is confined to your study."

Aroostine shook her head. The last thing she wanted to do was to hang around the building if she couldn't access her place. "I have my bank card on me, thank goodness. I'll just . . . stay with a friend." As she said the words, she realized she *did* have at least one friend in this miserable town.

She'd call Rosie from the back of a cab. They could recreate the work. Hell, her loss would inure to Rosie's benefit—she'd let the junior attorney take the lead on a witness or two. She really didn't have a choice. Not if she still planned to win this trial.

"Good luck," Pete Richards called after her as she trudged to the corner to hail a cab.

CHAPTER TEN

Rosie met Aroostine at the door of her Columbia Heights townhouse.

"Come in, it's cold out there," she said by way of greeting, pulling Aroostine inside.

Aroostine looked around and tried not to gape at the exposed brick walls, the orange and red canvas hanging over the fireplace, and the abundance of dark, rich wood and sumptuous fabrics.

"This is gorgeous. Did you do all this yourself?"

The townhome was the picture of urban sophistication.

Rosie blushed. "No. When I saved enough for a down payment for a house, my parents surprised me by hiring an interior designer to furnish it. They said I'd be living out of the IKEA as-is room forever on a government lawyer's salary. You know how it is, being young and single—I'm sure your family's the same way."

Young and single. A pang of guilt plucked at Aroostine's conscience. But she decided this wasn't the right time to mention to her closest friend in DC that, oh, by the way, she had a husband back home.

Instead, she focused on the notion of the Higgenses hiring a decorator and swallowed a giggle.

"Um, back home nobody really has their house decorated by a professional."

Rosie cocked her head. "Really?"

Aroostine thought of the roosters and folk art Americana that most of her parents' friends favored. They picked up their tchotchkes at the craft stalls that dotted the annual Apple Festival, not at some high-end, European furniture store.

"Really," she assured her friend.

"Huh. Anyway, speaking of being single—"

"Yeah?"

"Somebody was asking about you."

"Asking about *me*?"

"You have an admirer," Rosie teased.

Aroostine felt her face grow warm.

"Mitchell?" she guessed.

"You nailed it," Rosie confirmed. "He's cute—I think so, at least. I didn't even know he was single. He's always so serious and focused at work, we've never talked about his personal life. Not until *you* showed up, that is."

She wasn't sure how to respond. This was probably the best chance she'd have to mention the small matter of her marital status. But she really didn't feel like talking about Joe.

"Uh, so, I could really use a shower," she said, both because she was desperate to change the subject and because it was true.

"Oh, of course! I'm sorry. After the day you've had, I'm sure you could. Follow me."

Rosie led her up the narrow spiral staircase and down a short corridor.

"Here's the guest room. There should be towels and shampoo and stuff in the bathroom. I'll grab you a pair of sweats and leave them on the bed."

"Thank you, seriously, so much. But, um, I don't really think sweats are appropriate for the office, even on a Saturday," Aroostine said gently.

She gave Rosie's gray leggings and long-sleeved t-shirt a pointed look to suggest she might also want to change before they went into work.

Rosie cocked her head and looked bemused.

"What?" Aroostine asked.

"There is *no way* we're working today. We're going to hang out and relax, then eat Chinese takeout, watch girlie movies, and drink a bottle of good red wine."

Aroostine gave her the same look back.

"Are you crazy? One, we have jury selection in *six days*. Trial starts in nine days. I just lost all my notes, and Hernandez granted the motion *in limine*—which reminds me, did the Clerk's Office get back to you? Please tell me they did and the whole thing's been resolved."

"Not yet. The guy did say it would take him a while to research it. So I'm sure, eventually, it'll get straightened out."

"What's *a while*?"

Rosie chewed on her bottom lip for a few long seconds, then she admitted, "It could take as long as a week."

"A week? We don't have a week. That settles it: we're *definitely* not taking the day off."

"Oh, yes, we are," Rosie informed her.

Aroostine studied her silently.

"No way."

Rosie held her ground. "Listen, you're the boss, but this week has *sucked*—I mean, even without your place catching on fire, it sucked. The fire is just the cherry on this crap sundae. You deserve a day to recharge. No, strike that, you *need* a day to recharge. We'll get up at the crack of dawn and work all day tomorrow. Deal?"

Aroostine bit her lip and considered Rosie's plan. It *had* been a miserable week.

"Okay, but I don't drink."

"You do tonight," Rosie said, and her mouth curved into a grin.

Aroostine rolled her eyes and headed into the bathroom. She shoved her worries about the trial, Joe, and the ridiculous notion of a romance with Mitchell to the back of her head.

CHAPTER ELEVEN

Sunday morning

Aroostine held her identification badge up to the reader and waited for the soft click that signified the door had opened. She pushed it open and held it for Rosie.

Rosie was still grumbling about the early hour. She shook her head and dug her own badge out of her purse. "I don't think so, sister. If you're going to drag my butt in here before sunrise on a Sunday, you better believe Sid and all the bean counters are gonna know I was here. I want full credit."

She turned and waved at the security camera. "Hi, Sid!"

Aroostine couldn't suppress the laugh that rose in her throat. "You're insane."

She rolled her neck and stretched her back while she waited for Rosie to finish mugging for whoever had the bad luck to be monitoring the cameras at five thirty in the morning. To her infinite surprise, she didn't even have a headache. She'd fully expected to wake up hungover and sick after not one, but two, bottles of Syrah.

Instead, she felt rested and ready to tackle the mountain of work that awaited them. Maybe, she reasoned, every once in a while, a person just really needed a night of egg rolls, girl talk, and bad Lifetime movies.

The night had gotten a little fuzzy toward the end, though. She could only hope that she hadn't blurted out anything about Joe. Or, worse, Mitchell. She reddened at the thought.

Rosie followed her through the door, and Aroostine told herself to forget about her disastrous personal life and focus on the trial. It was time to get serious.

"Grab your laptop and meet me in the big conference room so we can spread out," she said to Rosie's back, as the younger attorney made a beeline for the kitchen.

"Caffeine first, you demon woman."

"Do what you need to do. I'll get the files."

"Do you want a mug of tea, at least?" Rosie called over her shoulder as Aroostine headed for her office.

"Sure, that'd be great."

She ducked into her dark office and scooped up several of the Redwelds that formed an unsteady tower on her desk. She eyed the trio of fat three-ring binders stacked alongside the desk and considered whether she could possibly manage to carry everything.

Deciding it wasn't worth it to try, she took the Redwelds and dumped them on the conference room table. She detoured to the supply closet to sign out a loaner laptop and dropped it off in the conference room, then headed back to retrieve the binders.

On her way through her office, she bumped the corner of her desk, knocking the heart-shaped paperweight to the floor.

She dropped the binders on the desk and bent to retrieve it, turning the cool, gray rock over in her hand. The memory of the day Joe gave it to her washed over her like a wave.

Joe and Rufus had spent a lazy August morning fishing in the stream out back. They came tromping into the kitchen just before lunchtime, both of them dripping water on the floor.

She'd looked up from her reading.

"Any luck?"

Joe grinned and hefted his cooler.

"Four trout."

"Nice."

She marked her place and walked over to take the cooler from him, wrinkling her nose. "One or both of you smells like wet dog. Why don't you take a shower while I clean these?"

He'd bent and planted a sweaty kiss near her ear. At the same time, he slipped something smooth and heavy into her hand and closed her fist around it. "We found this, too. Made me think of you."

And then he disappeared up the stairs, whistling, with Rufus trotting along behind him.

She'd opened her hand to find the perfectly heart-shaped stone, still wet from resting in the bed of the stream.

She lost track of time as she stood there turning the rock in her hands, her mind hundreds of miles away in her sunny kitchen.

Rosie appeared in the doorway.

"Hey, you okay?"

"What? Yeah—sorry." She forced herself back into the present, set the paperweight on the desk, and gestured to the binders. "Can you give me a hand with these?"

"Sure." She grabbed the top binder and eyed Aroostine closely. "Are you sure you're okay?"

Aroostine swallowed around the lump in her throat and searched her mind for a suitable lie. "Just trying to recreate my opening from memory, that's all. Let's go. We can divvy up the witnesses."

"Divvy them up? You mean . . . you're going to let me take a witness?"

Judging by the shock that glazed Rosie's face, her distraction effort had succeeded.

She smiled. "Maybe two," she tossed over her shoulder, as she walked out of the office with Rosie tripping on her heels.

First, though, they'd have to draft a motion to file their opposition *nunc pro tunc*, just in case Rosie's contact at the Clerk's Office couldn't figure out what happened and get the opposition reinstated. They wouldn't spend too much time on it—a motion *nunc pro tunc* was, at its core, a formality, a technicality. It was simply a way to correct a clerical error after the time for doing so had passed. No judge in the world, not even one harboring a grudge against a government lawyer, would refuse to grant it.

CHAPTER TWELVE

"What is it?"

Franklin pushed away his irritation at the greeting. He couldn't afford to get into a snit with the man on the other end of the phone—the man who held his mother's life in his hands.

"I wanted to give you an update."

"Please do."

"At exactly five thirty this morning, Aroostine Higgins's card registered on the log. Less than a minute later Rosalinda Montoya's card registered."

"And she is?"

"Montoya? Another lawyer at Justice. Junior to Higgins. Her name isn't on the signature block of the complaint, but she has signed some motions and certifications."

"So she is assigned to the trial?"

"I don't know. Possibly?"

"Is that all?"

Franklin checked the pocket-sized notebook he'd picked up at the dollar store near his home. If there was one thing he knew beyond a doubt, it was that every electronic file left *some* trace, no matter how crafty and careful its author believed himself to be. He'd decided any notes he took in the course of one of his so-called assignments would exist only in physical form. There would be no digital footprints leading back to him; more accurately, there would be no digital footprints that would make sense to anyone who hadn't invented the RemoteControl system.

"No. Higgins used her card to open the locked file room, while the other woman used hers to access the kitchen. The lights in conference room C were turned on, and both women signed on to their laptops from that space. They've been camped out in the conference room ever since."

"Have you been tracking all their activity?"

"To the extent possible, yes."

The man huffed in his ear, and Franklin heard a slapping sound, as if he'd struck his thigh or, God forbid, another person, in exasperation.

"And what extent would that be?" the man asked, his voice sarcastic and mocking.

"I can tell if one of them opens, modifies, or prints an existing file. And I can tell if one of them creates a new file. But I can't tell the exact letters or numbers they're typing," he answered carefully.

"Why not?"

"Um, that would require the installation of a keystroke logger. That could be done remotely, but it's probably a serious felony, like high treason or espionage or something, seeing as how they work for the Criminal Division of the federal government. Do you . . . Is that something you want?"

Franklin sent up a silent prayer that the man would say no.

There was a pause. Then the man said slowly, "No. Not yet, at least. What about e-mails?"

"Neither one has opened her e-mail yet."

"What information can you gather about the e-mails?"

"Oh, I can see everything on the e-mails. Envelope information—recipient, sender, subject, time, and date—as well as the content."

"You can read her e-mails but not her files?"

Franklin heard the disbelief in his voice and hurried to answer. "Yes. Look, I know it seems counterintuitive, but it's just a function of it being a different program. I can explain it, but it's highly technical. How much detail do you want?"

"None. Just make sure you capture all the information you can, whether or not it seems important to you."

"I will. In that case, you may also want to know that the Higgins woman has a dental appointment tomorrow morning."

Franklin tossed out the piece of information mainly because the man's insistence that he not use his judgment rankled him. Fine, let him sift through all the useless crap himself.

To his surprise, the man's voice registered excitement.

"She does? Where? What time?"

"Uh . . ." He checked his notes. "According to her Outlook calendar, she has a wisdom tooth extraction scheduled at Suburban Dental Surgery Associates with a Dr. Davis at eight o'clock tomorrow morning."

"Suburban? This office is associated with Suburban Hospital, yes?"

"I don't know."

"Find out. SystemSource has contracts with the hospital. See if your company provided a monitoring system to the dental surgery suite and call me back."

"But—"

"Do it."

The line went dead.

He stared down at the phone in his hand. How did the man know so much about SystemSource's business? Again, the worry that the man was someone from work nipped at him like a yappy little dog. He shook his head, there was no one with an accent like that at the company—at least no one he'd ever met. And, in the end, what difference did it make *who* he was? The man owned him, and that was all that really mattered now.

He opened the contracts database to perform the search the man wanted and ignored the fact that his fingers were shaking. He scanned the list of clients. His mother's kidnapper would be pleased to know that, as an affiliate of Suburban Hospital, Aroostine Higgins's oral surgeon did, in fact, use SystemSource's medical equipment monitoring system.

CHAPTER THIRTEEN

Monday morning

Franklin took a steadying breath to fight the nausea that had been coming over him in waves all morning.

When he'd called the man back to tell him that Suburban Dental Surgery Associates did use RemoteControl both to run its office network and to monitor the medical equipment in the surgical suites, the man had been elated. He ordered Franklin to interrupt the supplemental oxygen supply being delivered nasally and to cut power to the vital signs monitoring equipment once the lawyer's procedure was well underway. Then, he'd disconnected the call.

And Franklin had lain awake trying to rationalize what he'd be doing the next day. He'd argued with himself as he tossed, turned, and twisted in his bed.

It's just dental surgery—she won't be under general anesthesia. It's not like she's going to die. Is it?

He thought he'd stared at the ceiling all night, but he must have fallen asleep at some point, because he awoke to the sun streaming through his window with his face wet from the tears he'd shed during one of his dreams.

He called into the office to report that he was feeling ill (true enough) and planned to work from home for the next day or two. Then he brewed a pot of coffee and sat with a mug and stared at the clock on the kitchen wall.

At seven fifty, he imagined the lawyer arriving, dressed in a suit and eager to get her appointment out of the way and get on with her full day at the office. Although the dental office's notes indicated the recommended recovery time after a wisdom tooth extraction was at least twenty-four to thirty-six hours at home, Aroostine's Outlook calendar was packed with meetings on both Monday afternoon and all day Tuesday—all of them listed under the caption of her upcoming trial. He would have bet that she insisted on the first appointment of the day to accommodate her pretrial schedule. She probably thought there was no way she could spare the entire day—which was probably especially true now that her home computer had been destroyed in the fire.

At eight o'clock, he imagined her settling into the vinyl dental chair, possibly a touch nervous, to await the arrival of Dr. Davis. Franklin tried to distract himself by checking his e-mail, but he was too antsy to focus on the messages, so he closed the program and just sat, staring blankly at the screen until it went black, and waited.

At ten minutes after eight, his computer screen blinked to life; the program tracking the use of the medical equipment was active.

This is it. He stared at the information scrolling across the screen. Her vital signs were being monitored. And the cocktail of sedatives and painkillers was being delivered into her veins. He watched the display show that her heart rate and breathing had settled into a slow, steady rhythm, and the supplemental oxygen had begun to flow.

The procedure was underway. He'd give the oral surgeon time to make his first cuts.

He lifted his mug to his mouth and took a swig of coffee. Cold. Disgusting.

He stood to spit it into the sink. When he raised his head from the basin, his heart stopped. A black and white patrol car was parked in the alley directly at the end of his small yard.

His stomach seized. He grasped the edge of the counter to steady himself.

It was over. The police were coming for him. There was probably another car stationed out front. They were going to crash through his door and throw him to the floor.

He focused on breathing, which suddenly seemed like an almost impossibly difficult task.

A knock sounded on the kitchen door.

He swallowed but couldn't seem to convince his legs to move to the door.

His mother was going to die because, somehow, somewhere, he'd slipped up.

Another knock, more insistent this time.

He craned his neck to look through the window and see how many of them were out there.

What he saw was Tyrone Johnson in his patrolman's uniform, raising a hand to knock on his kitchen door a third time, a deep frown of irritation creasing his mouth.

What had Tyrone learned? Did he know?

Tyrone rapped loudly against the door.

Franklin forced his numb legs to move in the direction of the sound.

He stood in front of the door and worked up some saliva to wet his throat. Then he pulled it open.

Tyrone was pulling his radio from his belt.

"Oh, good. You're alive."

"Why wouldn't I be?" Franklin croaked.

"I dunno, man. It's been quiet over here. No one's seen your ma in days. And your lights have been on twenty-four/seven. I thought maybe you bought it. Didn't want her to come back from her trip to visit your great-aunt and find your decomposing corpse, you know?"

Tyrone flashed him a smile, but Franklin got the distinct feeling that his neighbor didn't completely buy the great-aunt story.

"Heh," he chuckled weakly. "I've been working from home. I caught some kind of bug. Flu maybe? Anyway, that's the benefit of working in IT. I can do it in my pajamas from my kitchen table."

Tyrone's eyes flitted from Franklin's face and swept through the visible portion of the house.

Franklin moved into the doorway to block the cop's ingress and continued, "So, uh, not to be rude, but I don't want to give you whatever I've got. It's nasty."

"You working 'round the clock?"

"What?"

"The lights? Your lights are on all night long."

"Oh. Uh, actually, it's this stomach flu. I've running back and forth to the bathroom all night. It's bad, man. Sorry if the lights are bothering you and Gloria. I can turn them off tonight."

"No, don't sweat it." Tyrone's mouth curled into a sneer of disgust at the thought of his neighbor's stomach problems. "Just glad to know you didn't kick the bucket."

"Ha, yeah. Well, thanks for checking on me," Franklin said.

Tyrone was already backing away, like he was worried Franklin might projectile vomit on him or crap his pants right there in the doorway.

Franklin half-thought he might, too. But Tyrone left, and he swung the door shut and bolted it. Then he leaned against it and caught his breath.

It had been stupid to leave the lights on. It was an empty security gesture, anyway—a lame attempt to make himself feel better. But it had been reckless. He couldn't afford to draw that kind of attention to himself. The man had said if he talked to the police, his mother was as good as dead. He had to assume that he was being watched.

God, you're an idiot, he berated himself.

He stayed there, leaning against the door, until his pulse rate returned to normal. Then he remembered his assignment, and his pulse spiked again.

He whipped his head around and looked at the clock. It was almost eight thirty.

He had no idea how long the surgery would take, but the dental practice's schedule had the surgeon's next patient booked for nine o'clock.

He had to interrupt the oxygen flow and disrupt the vital signs monitoring before the dentist finished up. He didn't want to imagine what might happen to his mother if he didn't.

He ran across the kitchen to the table, sliding across the slick tile in his socks, and clicked his computer mouse frantically until the screen came to life. His eyes scanned the information as to which pieces of equipment were in use. With shaking fingers, he typed a line of code and hit "Enter."

Then, drained, he slumped into his chair and prayed he'd been quick enough.

Dr. Davis blinked and pulled back. His blue eyes widened with concern above the paper mask covering the lower part of his face. He wrinkled his brow and turned toward the instrument panel.

In her not-awake, not-asleep state, Aroostine could hear him whispering back and forth with a nurse she couldn't see. Whatever they were consulting about, she wished they'd hurry up. She didn't have time to sit here while these two chitchatted. She had work to do.

The whispering continued.

Her jaw was beginning to ache from hanging open.

Should she be able to feel her jaw?

The nurse floated across Aroostine's field of vision, a blur of colorful, patterned scrubs. Warm fingers on her pulse.

"How are you doing, honey?"

The nurse's face, calm but intent, swam into view.

Aroostine couldn't answer, what with her mouth cranked open like the hood of a car. So she tried to nod. Wasn't sure she succeeded.

She swallowed. She suddenly felt hot. And breathless.

Oh my God, I can't breathe. I can't breathe!

The nurse must have seen the panic in her eyes.

"It's okay," she soothed. "There's been a little . . . blip . . . with the machines. Just a hiccup. We'll get that oxygen flowing in a jiffy. You just stay calm and take deep, slow breaths. You hear me now?"

Aroostine nodded.

The nurse's face disappeared.

A cold metal stethoscope slipped under the paper sheet and settled on Aroostine's chest. She closed her eyes and tried to ignore the feeling that her throat was closing.

The beaver looked at her over its glossy shoulder and then turned back to the water, thumping its hind leg. It wanted her to follow it. It slipped into the cold stream and surged forward. She did the same. They darted through the water, twin sleek animals.

The beaver stopped in the long grass and looked up the bank to the woods. Beyond the trees, there it was: that small log house with the yellow square of light in the window.

She crouched in the shallow stream, water dripping off her hair and onto her shoulders and watched the house for what felt like hours. No one came. No one left. At some point, the beaver glided away. But Aroostine sat and watched. Waiting for something, but she didn't know what.

Bright, hot light seeped under her eyelids, and she jerked her head to the side, away from the assault.

"Aroostine? Can you hear me?"

She tried to swallow. Her mouth felt like it was full of cotton. Her head ached. Her face hurt.

She forced her eyes open, wincing at the light.

Dr. Davis hovered over her.

The surgery, she remembered. It must be over.

Time to go to work.

She struggled to sit up and shivered in the cold room.

"Are we done? I have a meeting," she asked thickly, trying to push herself out of the chair and onto her feet.

He put a gentle hand on her chest and pressed her back into the chair.

"Slow down. You aren't going anywhere just yet."

She wet her lips and tried to find her voice to protest.

"Listen to me, Ms. Higgins. Please. There was an . . . event . . . during your procedure."

An event?

She stared at him and waited for clarification.

He cleared his throat and continued. "It appears that the supplemental oxygen delivery system failed. It's unprecedented, actually. And to compound the problem, the system that monitors your vital signs went dark, too."

"Wha—?"

He held up a hand to cut her off. "Please stay calm. You're fine. Nurse Loomis monitored your heart rate and breathing manually while I finished off your stitches. Fortunately, we were nearly done when the equipment failed."

Aroostine relaxed against the chair. Everything was fine.

A wrinkle creased Dr. Davis's brow, and he straightened the tie under his white lab coat.

"I do need to tell you, however, that you did go into shock briefly."

Or not so fine.

"Now, that may not have been related to the equipment failure," he said, the cadence of his voice morphing from reassuring doctor talking to his patient to robotic litigation avoider.

She raised an eyebrow—or thought she did. It was impossible to know, seeing as how she couldn't really feel her face.

"Some people react negatively to the sedative. Your blood pressure may have plummeted as a result of some complex reaction you had, which we couldn't have predicted or planned for."

She concentrated on forming the words and managed to croak them out. "It seems pretty clear that the simplest explanation is whatever happened to me was a result of your equipment failure."

Although she kept her raspy voice even, he stiffened as though she'd threatened him.

"I don't think that's a fair statement. Your procedure was successful, and you can be sure the office will be investigating the cause of the equipment failure. Now, I suggest you follow Nurse Loomis to the front desk and get your painkiller prescription and discharge papers, so you can go home and get some rest."

He walked out of the room so quickly Aroostine half-expected him to break into a jog.

The nurse hovered awkwardly by the door, clutching a plastic bag that appeared to hold Aroostine's clothes.

"Here are your things. Why don't you get dressed, and I'll walk you out. I'll wait for you in the hall, unless you think you'll need help."

Aroostine wet her cracked lips. "I can manage on my own, thanks."

She waited until the door clicked shut and then pulled on her pantsuit and jammed her feet into her shoes. Despite the oral surgeon's advice, she had no intention of going home. She had too much work to do to spend the day curled up in bed feeling sorry for herself. By rights, she should have rescheduled the appointment when Judge Hernandez moved up the trial, but it had taken six weeks to get on Dr. Davis's schedule in the first place, and the teeth had been bothering her for months. Having decided to go through with the surgery, she couldn't burn an entire workday recovering. She'd just have to power through the pain.

She combed her fingers through her thick hair and slung her purse over her shoulder.

"All set?" the nurse chirped as Aroostine stepped out into the hall.

Aroostine nodded mutely and trailed the nurse along the thickly carpeted hallway to the front of the office. Speaking was too much effort.

The nurse caught the receptionist's eye and nodded toward Aroostine. "Okay, Lindsay, Ms. Higgins here is ready to check out."

She disappeared around the corner before the receptionist could ask any questions.

Lindsay looked up from her computer monitor and smiled brightly at Aroostine. Her fingers flew over the keys, and she scanned the screen. The smile vanished.

"Do you have someone coming to pick you up?" she asked in a tone that suggested she already knew the answer.

"No."

"I'm sorry, but I can't let you leave on your own."

Aroostine dug through the fog that had settled over her brain and pulled out a memory. "We worked this out beforehand. I'm alone here. I don't have anyone who can come get me. Especially with no notice."

Lindsay gave her a pitying look, but her voice was officious and firm. "I see here in the notes that you did ask us to make an exception to that policy."

Aroostine nodded.

The receptionist continued. "Dr. Davis has decided that, in light of today's . . . situation, we can't waive that requirement, after all."

Interesting that Dr. Davis hadn't bothered to tell her that.

She tried to summon her inner attorney. She knew she should be able to unleash a stream of well-chosen fifty-cent words intended to intimidate the woman behind the counter into letting her go. But suddenly, her will to argue evaporated; she didn't have the energy to whip herself into a frenzy. Instead, she mumbled Rosie's office number and sank into the nearest chair. She leaned her head back and closed her eyes to wait.

She started awake. A gentle hand was shaking her shoulder.

She blinked up, expecting to see Rosie. Instead, she met Mitch's worried eyes.

"Hey, sleepyhead, let's get out of here," he said in a voice barely above a whisper.

She tried to clear her head and get her bearings.

"Where's Rosie?" she asked, pushing herself out of the chair and reaching for her bag.

He was too quick for her. He slung the bag over his shoulder with one hand and steered her toward the door with the other.

"When the receptionist told Rosie what happened, I volunteered to get you. I have my car today, and you're in no shape to be taking the Metro."

He guided her along the hallway and pressed the elevator button.

She blinked painfully at the bright overhead lights.

"I'm fine," she protested.

"You're not fine. You almost died."

Her mouth was cottony. *God, she was parched. She'd give anything for a glass of water.*

"I don't think it was quite that dramatic," she managed.

He shot her a look and reached into his overcoat pocket. As if by magic, he produced a miniature bottle of Evian that he'd clearly snagged from the office kitchen.

"I thought you might be thirsty," he said as she snatched the bottle from his outstretched hand and took a greedy swallow.

The elevator bell rang, and the doors parted.

"Thank you so much. You have no idea," she said, finishing the bottle as he followed her into the empty elevator."

"Actually, I have some idea. I've had my wisdom teeth out. I remember how thirsty I was afterward."

"This is normal, then?"

"The thirst? Yeah. The almost dying part? No."

She gave him a grateful smile for the water, ignored the rest of it, and rested her head against the back of the elevator car. They rode in silence the rest of the way down to the lobby.

He offered her an arm as they walked through the front doors to the parking lot, but she shook her head. She had too much work to do. She couldn't act like an invalid. She wrapped her scarf around her neck and scrunched herself deep into her down jacket.

Luckily, his car was parked in one of the closest spots.

She settled in the passenger seat and blew into her hands to warm them. He started the engine and cranked the heat.

"It'll warm up soon."

"Thanks. I've been cold ever since the surgery."

"I'll bet. So, what's the best route to your apartment from here? Should I just go down Georgia Avenue?" he asked, checking his rearview mirror and putting the car into reverse to back out of the spot.

"My apartment? I'm not going home," she answered slowly, not fully understanding the question. "I'm going back to the office with you."

"No, you're not."

Her confusion turned to irritation.

"Yes, I am."

He put the car back into park and sighed. Then he shifted in his seat and pierced her with a serious gaze.

"Listen to me. Whether you want to believe it or not, you nearly died. The receptionist told Rosie you stopped breathing, your pulse rate plummeted, and your heart almost stopped beating. So, while it would have simply been a stupid, masochistic idea to come into the office after a routine wisdom tooth extraction, coming to work after what your body's been through is out of the question. I'm not taking you to the office."

She reached for the door handle.

Fine. She'd take a cab.

"And," he continued, "Sid said if you turn up today, he'll drag you out of there himself and take you home."

She froze.

"You told Sid?"

"He overheard me and Rosie talking. Now will you please stop being so macho and just give me your freaking address."

She stared at him for a long moment, her anger rising. He stared back.

She swallowed hard and tried not to cry. She was too weak to get out of the car and storm off, so she mumbled the cross streets and settled back into the passenger seat.

The truth was, she didn't feel up to doing much more than curling up in her bed.

One day of rest, she promised herself. *And then it's full steam ahead.*

She realized she'd made that same promise just two days ago at Rosie's place. Having coworkers who cared about her was starting to interfere with her productivity.

CHAPTER FOURTEEN

Franklin jiggled his left leg while he watched the notes populate the entry for the lawyer's surgery in the oral surgical center's database. The words appeared slowly, on some sort of delay, several letters at a time.

Only when the entry was complete did he allow himself to exhale.

She was going to be fine.

She's going to be fine, he repeated to himself. The stomach-churning nausea that had gripped him since morning abated, and his body began to shake with relief.

He gripped his head with both hands.

He'd nearly killed her. When the device monitoring her heart rate had flatlined, he'd stared at the screen in disbelief. Then her pulse had dropped to nothing.

It had been just a blip. A moment. But the woman had almost died.

He had almost killed her, his brain screamed at him silently.

His eyes fell on the blue and green skeins of yarn that sat on the floor in a wicker basket near his mother's favorite chair, the knitting needles poking through the balls like chopsticks, waiting for her to start a sweater or scarf or whatever her next project was supposed to be.

I don't have a choice, he told himself. The words dug into his skull like claws. He had no choice.

He and his mother were entirely at the mercy of the faceless, nameless monster who had grabbed her. And that meant Aroostine Higgins was too.

Think.

He scrubbed his face with his hands. He just needed to think of a way out of this. He reminded himself he had a fine analytic mind. If he attacked this impossible dilemma like a puzzle or a math problem, he could solve it. He had to.

The shrill chirp of the prepaid cell phone interrupted his musing. And his nausea returned like a punch in the gut.

"Hello?" He couldn't keep the dread out of his voice.

"Hello, Franklin."

The man waited.

"Um, what can I do for you?" Franklin asked, afraid to hear the answer.

"A report, you idiot," the man finally huffed. "I'm calling for a report on the surgery."

"Oh." In his panic, Franklin had completely forgotten to call in. Now, his fear spiked. "I'm so sorry. I was just about to call you." The words tumbled out in a desperate rush.

"It's no matter," the man said in an oddly soothing tone. "Your mother's fingers should heal fine."

"Her fingers? Heal?" He couldn't make sense of the words so he simply repeated them.

"Yes, her broken fingers. You should have called me two hours ago. You did not. And now, your mother has two broken fingers."

Oh God. No.

"I'm afraid so."

Franklin hadn't realized he'd spoken aloud until the monster on the other end of the phone answered him.

"Can I . . . Can I talk to her? Please?"

"She's indisposed."

"Please!"

"Let's focus, shall we? What happened with the attorney? Did you do as I directed?"

Franklin's mind spun. He took great gulps of breath and tried to ignore the image that his brain had constructed of his mother cradling her hand, grimacing in pain, two fingers sticking out at odd angles.

"Yes. Yes, I did. According to the surgery notes, the interruption caused her body to go into shock. She's going to be fine. She was released with instructions to go home and rest. She hasn't used her card to access the office, so, apparently, she followed doctor's orders."

"Very good."

Franklin's stomach turned at the satisfaction in the man's voice.

"She could have died."

"That's not your concern."

Not his concern? Was he joking?

"It'll be my concern if I'm an accomplice to murder. Maybe I should turn myself in now, before someone else gets hurt, or worse," he shot back before he could stop himself.

He gripped the phone and waited for the explosion he was sure would come.

Instead, the man laughed. When he finally spoke, he sounded genuinely amused.

"Accomplice? Accomplice to whom, Franklin? I'm no one. A ghost. A specter. What will you tell the police—the mystery man on the phone told you to do it? You might as well blame the voices in your head. No, Franklin. You can wipe the idea of involving the authorities from your mind. And, rather than worrying about some attorney who is a stranger to you, your energy would be better spent thinking of the woman who gave you life and raised you, don't you agree? Your mother's survival is in your hands."

Franklin's stomach lurched as he considered the man's words. He was trapped. He was a hostage, no different from his mother.

"May I please speak to her?" he croaked through suddenly dry lips.

"Perhaps tomorrow. If you earn the privilege."

The sudden *click* of the call disconnecting echoed in his ear like a shot. He stared blankly at the wall. He was caught in a nightmare with no way out. He had to create an exit. Somehow.

CHAPTER FIFTEEN

Tuesday afternoon

Aroostine tried to still her trembling hands and stared down at the words swimming on the paper a process server had just shoved at her as she exited the elevator.

Her day had started out lousy—she'd forced herself into the office at her usual time, despite her aching mouth—only to find that Judge Hernandez had summarily denied her motion *nunc pro tunc* almost the instant Rosie had filed it. That news had stunned her, but she'd told herself at least her day had nowhere to go but up.

Judging by the document in her hands, she couldn't have been more wrong. She blinked as if the words might change.

Joseph C. Jackman v. Aroostine Higgins, Complaint in Divorce.

Her stomach lurched.

Don't throw up, don't throw up, she told herself as she worked up enough saliva to swallow.

Joe was divorcing her? Joe was divorcing her.

She leaned back against the wall across from her office door and blinked as hard as she could to stem the tide of thick tears that threatened to fall at any moment. If she could just get inside, she could have her impending breakdown in private.

She took a deep breath, put her head down, and stepped toward her door on unsteady legs.

Her legs buckled under her, and she felt herself riding a wave of humiliation to the floor.

Great. Just great.

And then warm hands grabbed her under her armpits and held her up.

"Easy there," said a concerned male voice, as its owner lifted her back to her feet.

She closed her eyes and willed herself to disappear.

"Aroostine?" Mitchell asked.

Crap. She hadn't disappeared.

She opened her eyes to see him staring at her with concern.

"Are you okay?"

She forced her mouth into an approximation of a smile.

"I'm fine. Thanks for catching me. I just . . . got light-headed. I guess maybe I should have stayed home one more day, after all," she lied. She rolled the divorce papers into a tube so he couldn't see the caption.

He raised an eyebrow at that. He and Rosie had been in a complete uproar when she'd shown up for work as usual. Apparently, they thought she'd just waste the final week of trial prep curled up on her couch, nursing her swollen mouth.

To his credit, he didn't bother to say "I told you so." Instead, he moved his hands to her back and gently guided her through her office door and deposited her in her chair.

Then he picked up her desk phone and punched in an internal extension.

"What are you doing? I'm fine, honestly," she insisted.

He held up a finger to silence her, then said, "Rosie? This is Mitch. Your first chair just collapsed in the hallway. I guess no one told you the junior attorney's responsible for keeping the trial team healthy? Bring her a cup of tea or something. And a bowl of soup—I'm sure she didn't bother with lunch."

He ended the call and smiled at Aroostine. "Help is on the way."

"Thanks. Really, thank you. But that wasn't very nice to Rosie. She's going to feel responsible."

She opened her top desk drawer and jammed the papers into it.

He cocked his head. "She knows I'm just giving her a hard time, and she clearly cares about you." He sat on the edge of the desk, his legs dangling just beside her chair, and lowered his voice. "We both do. Are you sure you don't want to talk about whatever's really going on?"

She felt trapped by his proximity and by the question. He seemed to be genuinely worried and interested. But there was no way she was going to tell the cute guy who worked in the next office about her failed marriage.

"I told you. I overdid it. And, you're right, I skipped lunch."

She lifted her chin and met his eyes, daring him to push it further. He didn't.

He sighed. "Take better care of yourself."

He pushed off the desk and stepped past her.

"Thanks again for the hand," she said to his back as he left the office.

He didn't respond but pulled her door shut on his way out.

She waited a full minute before yanking open the desk drawer and retrieving the divorce complaint.

She smoothed the wrinkled pages and licked her lips, putting off the inevitable for another few seconds.

She read the sterile boilerplate language with her heart banging in her ears. Joe's lawyer—and at least he'd had the decency to get an out-of-town attorney—had filed a very simple, no-fault divorce complaint. He asked the court to dissolve the marriage because it was "irretrievably broken."

The dispassionate document made no reference to the years they'd spent renovating the old farmhouse on the edge of town, room by room, the walks through the woods with their dog, the nights they'd passed in a blur of candles, tangled sheets, and intertwined limbs. Just a polite request to declare their relationship dead and beyond repair. Heavy tears fell on the papers before she could stop them.

Rosie rapped softly on the door and then cracked it open.

As she stepped quietly into the office, balancing a tray of food, Aroostine flipped the papers over so they were facedown on the desk and wiped her face with the back of her hand.

"Hey, I brought you some tomato bisque and a cup of tea. Do you need anything else?" Rosie asked in a solicitous voice.

She crossed the room and arranged the food like an offering to the gods, just so, in front of Aroostine.

"No, this is great. And thanks, Rosie. Mitchell shouldn't have called you like that. You didn't need to run downstairs for me."

Rosie waved a hand at the clumsy attempt at an apology.

"Don't be stupid. You need to eat. You really shouldn't have come in today."

"Well, thank you, anyway." She picked up the spoon and hoped Rosie would take the hint and leave before she started to cry again.

"Don't mention it."

Rosie turned to leave, then hesitated and shifted back around to look at Aroostine.

"What?"

"Nothing. Just . . . um, I thought you ate before we met to go over the exhibits?"

Aroostine gnawed on her inner cheek and tried to think quickly. She was a *terrible* liar. And she'd forgotten that she'd told Rosie she was going to grab a bite earlier.

"I was going to, but I got pulled into a meeting with Sid. That was stupid. I should have at least eaten a yogurt or something, huh?"

"Oh. Yeah, I guess."

Rosie gave her a quizzical look before she walked away.

Aroostine dropped the spoon on the desk. Food was the furthest thing from her mind.

She checked the time on her phone's display. *4:50 p.m.*

Joe would just be finishing up for the day. His clothes would be covered in wood shavings after spending hours sanding and smoothing reclaimed barn planks to turn into hand-crafted coffee tables, bookcases, and dressers for rich Northeasterners who wanted authentic, one-of-a-kind furnishings for their weekend country homes.

The late afternoon light streaming through the big, leaded glass windows would bounce off of his slightly-too-long blond hair when he bent down to pet Rufus and wake him up for the short walk from the workshop back to the house.

A pain seared her chest.

Dammit, Joe.

Her hand hovered over the phone. She took several deep breaths and tried to quell the roiling feeling in her stomach. Then, before she could lose her nerve, she called his cell phone.

Four rings. Then his voicemail picked up. She told herself he probably had his music up too loud and didn't hear the phone. The alternative was too ugly to consider.

The device beeped in her ear, and she made no effort to hide the pain in her voice when she left her message:

"Hey, it's me. I got the divorce papers today. We need to talk. Call me, please." She hesitated, then added, "I love you."

She dropped the handset back onto the receiver with a shaking hand and set her mouth in a firm line. She'd done what she could. Now she had to put Joe out of her mind and focus on the trial.

Eight miles away, Franklin Chang clicked on a set of coordinates with his own shaking hand.

"Gotcha," he muttered under his breath, tracing the call the attorney had just placed to a mobile number assigned to a small town in Pennsylvania.

He opened another window and typed in a code, checking first to ensure that his monitor's privacy screen was active.

In less than a second, the subscriber's name and other identifying information scrolled across the screen: Joseph Charles Jackman, age twenty-six, married to one Aroostine Higgins. Mr. Jackman's address, place of business, social security number, and Pennsylvania driver's license number followed.

Bingo. A surge of excitement shot up his spine.

He stared at the screen for a long moment and memorized the words and numbers, thankful—not for the first time—for his photographic memory. This wasn't something he wanted to write down, not even in the notebook. He didn't ever want this information to be traced back to him.

He jumped to his feet and fumbled around in his pocket for the cell phone.

He paced in a circle while he placed his call. This was it. His mother's ticket home.

The man answered on the third ring.

"What?"

"I have something. Something big. But if I give it to you, you have to release my mother."

The man snorted. "You're in no position to make demands."

"Actually, you're wrong."

"I don't have time for these games. Perhaps your mother doesn't need the use of her hand at all, eh?"

"No, listen to me. Aroostine Higgins is married, and I can give you her husband."

A low, appreciative whistle sounded in Franklin's ear.

"Well done."

"But I'm not going to unless you agree to let my mother go." He edged his voice with steel.

A long silence followed.

He waited.

And waited.

He was beginning to worry he'd been too forceful and missed his opportunity, when the man said, "Fine."

Fine. One terse, clipped word that would save his mother's life.

"Thank you. Let me speak to her."

"The information first, Franklin. And then you may talk to her. You have my word."

He hesitated for a moment, and then the information that he'd seared into his brain spilled out in a rush of numbers, letters, and jumbled words.

"Stop," the man demanded.

Franklin stopped.

"Now, slowly, begin again, please, and explain how you came to know all this."

Franklin gulped and forced himself to speak calmly despite his racing pulse and pounding heart. "The lawyer placed a personal call just now. I've been monitoring her incoming and outgoing calls, just like you wanted, to see if there was anything you could use."

"Very good. Go on."

"She left a message at this number regarding divorce papers."

"She is married? And they are estranged?"

"Apparently."

There was silence on the other end of the phone. Franklin took a moment to feel sorry for whichever henchman had failed to uncover these basic vital statistics. He assumed both that there were many henchmen, and that they were maimed—or possibly killed—whenever they screwed up. This belief, combined with his constant concern and worry about his mother, had completely destroyed his ability to sleep and eat. But that was all about to end.

"And she is divorcing her husband?"

"No, it sounded more like he is divorcing her. She seemed upset and surprised." Franklin scrolled through his memory to recall the message she'd left. "She asked him to call her. Said she loved him."

"This is interesting. You've done well. Repeat the information now, and as I promised, you may talk to your mother."

Franklin closed his eyes and sent up a silent prayer of gratitude before rattling off the information the man would need to do whatever it was he planned to do to Joseph C. Jackman. He regretted what might happen to him, but he had his own priorities.

He heard shuffling and murmured voices, then the man activated the speakerphone.

His mother's soft voice was in his ear.

"Franklin?"

"Mom, are you okay?"

"I'm fine, honey."

"No you're not. He told me he broke your fingers."

"Oh, that. It was nothing." She scoffed.

In the background, Franklin could hear the man muttering darkly.

"Mom, don't say that—don't challenge him."

His mother sighed. "It doesn't matter. He's going to do what he's going to do."

"It's over. I got him what he wanted, and he's going to let you go!"

She sighed softly. "Oh, honey, no he's not."

"He is," he insisted. "We have a deal."

His mother's voice was gentle but insistent. "I don't think this is a gentleman who honors his agreements. I think I'm going to die in this cabin. Just remember, I love you very much."

He shook his head as if she could see him. "Don't talk that way—"

"Playtime's over, Junior," the man's deep voice said, replacing his mother's refined one. "I have work to do. And so do you."

"Wait. I'm done. You're going to let my mother go. You said you would."

The man laughed, an ugly, black laugh. "There's been a change of plans."

He was still laughing when he hung up on Franklin.

CHAPTER SIXTEEN

Joe told himself to delete the voicemail—or, at a minimum, stop playing it over and over. And yet, he couldn't seem to help himself. He hit the "1" key again to replay it.

The sadness. The hesitation. And then the little hitch in her voice before she said she loved him.

Rufus whined up at him and pawed at his ears.

"Sorry, boy. I'll stop." He heard the catch in his own voice and cleared his throat.

He balled his hands into fists and then released them, reaching down to scratch the dog's head absently.

He'd known serving Aroostine with the divorce papers would prompt her to contact him. He also knew the decent thing would have been to at least call her and warn her that he'd filed the complaint. But more than that, he knew that if he spoke to her, he'd lose his resolve. Hell, he'd been unable to pull the trigger on starting the process for weeks.

So, fueled by liquid courage after his night out with Brent, he'd scrawled his name above the signature line, shoved the papers into the envelope his attorney had helpfully provided, then stumbled along the iced-over path down to the mailbox at the end of the driveway and stuffed the envelope inside.

He'd slept past ten the next morning, and only woke, with a mouth full of cotton and a throbbing headache, when Rufus had become loudly insistent about his need to go outside.

As he shivered in his flannel shirt while Rufus watered the bushes, he suddenly remembered what he'd done. Regret flamed in his mind, and he raced to the mailbox to retrieve the papers.

It was too late. The little red flag was down, and when he pulled open the box, he found a fresh stack of catalogs and utility bills. The divorce complaint was gone, on its way to the Law Offices of J. Patrick Townsley, Esquire, who would serve it on Aroostine and file it with the court.

For a wild moment, he considered calling the lawyer and telling him he'd changed his mind. Then he told himself it was for the best. For him and Aroostine both.

And since that moment in his driveway, he'd steadfastly refused to think about what came next. Every time the thought of divorce popped into his mind, he'd pushed it away.

But now what came next was here, and it hit him in the gut like a cold, steel fist. He gasped and bent over, clutching his knees with his hands.

Rufus whimpered.

Joe tried to swallow, but he couldn't. His chest was being squeezed by an unseen hand. For a long moment, he panicked, convinced he was having a heart attack, but the feeling passed as quickly as it had come.

Don't fall apart, he ordered himself. He'd chosen this course, and now he had to stay it.

He put away his tools and cleared the wood scraps from his

workbench methodically. He worked quickly and efficiently, falling into a rhythm. The familiar routine calmed him, and his heartbeat slowed to normal.

He had to keep busy, that's all. As long as he didn't allow himself to dwell on the wreckage of his marriage, he'd be just fine.

In fact, he decided, he knew exactly how to distract himself. He'd take Rufus back to the house and feed him his dinner, then head over to the Hole in the Wall for Two-fer Tuesday. Two beers for two bucks sounded like the prescription for what ailed him. And he'd leave his blasted cell phone at home, so he wouldn't be tempted to make a late-night call that he'd regret.

Maybe, just maybe, he'd even strike up a conversation with that friendly barmaid. The redhead with freckles and a smile the size of Ohio.

He left a voicemail for Brent in case he wanted to meet him at the bar and whistled to let Rufus know it was time to go.

⸻

Jen checked her notes. This was the place. She'd gotten the assignment twenty minutes earlier and had sped to the address. Apparently, she'd beat the target to the location because she saw no sign of the guy or his vehicle.

She passed the time listening to played-out country songs on the radio. Just as Shania started caterwauling about boots under a bed, the target drove past and slowed to make a right turn.

He parked a dusty American-made pickup in the lot behind the town's bar, which appeared to live down to its name. It was every inch of a dive, from the windowless facade to the bent and weathered board stuck in the cement out front advertising two-for-one drafts.

The guy hopped from the truck's cab and turned up the collar of his tan jacket before heading into the wind and trudging across the parking lot, which was nearly filled with dusty American-made pickup trucks—F-150s mainly. He was alone.

From her spot in front of the gas station across the street, Jen watched from the warmth of her own F-150 until he disappeared into the bar. Then she flipped down the visor above the dash and checked her makeup in the illuminated mirror.

She winced at the way the skin under her eyes was beginning to wrinkle and sag. The lines and the sallow color were unavoidable effects of working nights. It aged a girl.

A quick coat of lip gloss and a hair fluffing later, she zipped up her leather jacket and killed the engine.

The Silk Road gig had specified a low-key approach, nothing overtly sexy. She was glad she'd paid attention to the details. This joint looked like a tight jeans and clingy sweater kind of place. Her usual club attire of low-cut dresses and sparkly tank tops would have stuck out.

Whatever.

The atmosphere might be low-rent, but the job promised to pay top dollar. If she pulled this off, she'd have enough bitcoins in her account that she wouldn't have to work the truck stop parking lot for, like, the rest of the year. She might even be able to afford some pricey skin cream to take care of those wrinkles.

And, in a nice change of pace, she wouldn't even have to screw this loser. Just deliver him to the agreed-upon location. Although, truth be told, he wasn't hard on the eyes. He looked like he worked out, and his jeans hugged his butt nicely. Maybe she'd do a little freelancing before she handed him over—it might be nice to be with someone whose gut didn't sag over his pants.

She pulled open her purse to make sure the bottle of roofies was in easy reach and patted the vial of pills for luck. She would wait long enough for the guy to get himself seated and settled in with a drink, then she'd head across the highway and work her magic.

CHAPTER SEVENTEEN

To Joe's disappointment, the bubbly redhead wasn't working. Instead, when he pushed the steel door inward, he was greeted by Mikey's ugly mug.

"Joe." The bartender nodded and turned back to the hockey action on the wall-mounted television.

Joe settled onto a stool and looked around the narrow, dimly-lit bar. It was already crowded with bargain-hunting couples and buddies taking advantage of the two-for-one drink deal.

He felt conspicuous, alone in a sea of pairs.

The announcers threw it to commercial, and Mikey walked over to take Joe's order.

"Two lagers?"

He almost said yes but considered a moment and said, "Nah. Two stouts." There was no need to specify a brand—only Yuengling qualified for the two-for-one deal. Not that anyone in town drank anything else anyway. He didn't know why the place bothered to stock other labels.

An eyebrow crawled up Mikey's face.

"Thought Aroostine didn't like you drinking during the week."

Aroostine didn't like him drinking, period. And she hated the Hole in the Wall. But he had no intention of getting into a discussion about Aroostine's views with Mikey.

"Lucky the second one's not for her then, huh?"

Mikey chuckled and flicked his bar rag over his shoulder as he walked away.

Joe didn't want to bad-mouth his wife, especially because it would just be a matter of time before the entire town of Walnut Bottom knew about the divorce. But, all the same, he figured that he no longer needed to honor her views about drinking and slumming it in a place like this.

Not that he could really fault her. She'd come by her opinions the hard way. The whole reason she'd been adopted out of her tribe was that her parents had literally drunk themselves to death. Her grandfather, who'd pretty much raised her anyway, had made arrangements for a childless couple he knew from town to take care of her after he died. The old man had taken a keen look at the way the culture was disintegrating and decided his granddaughter would be better off away from her heritage.

He'd been right, too, Joe mused, as he hoisted the only slightly dirty mug to his lips. The Higginses had given Aroostine a stable home, support, and a good start in life. She'd grown up surrounded by love. They'd adopted her when she was seven, and if you ran into them around town, they'd still just about burst with pride to tell you how successful and smart she was.

Joe loved her ambition, he really did. But she was just so serious and driven, always moving forward, never slowing down. He didn't want to live in the fast lane, especially not cooped up like a chicken in some concrete pen.

He drained the glass and returned it to the bar with a dull thud.

The whole point was *not* to think about his soon-to-be ex-wife. Or her glossy curtain of hair. Her soft lips. Her silvery laugh.

"Mikey. Let's have the other one now." He gestured toward the empty mug and hoped the barkeep wouldn't notice the thick emotion in his voice.

A blast of cold air hit the back of his neck as the steel door to the bar opened inward. He didn't turn to greet the newcomer because he was studiously avoiding looking to his right, where Kirk Galeton was regaling the checkout girl from the Stop-n-Shop with tales of his quarterbacking prowess. Having graduated high school with Kirk, Joe was fairly certain Kirk had thrown his last touchdown pass before his rapt listener had graduated from diapers, but who was he to judge?

The arrival of the second beer coincided with that of a stranger. A curvy bottle-blonde, who squeezed herself in between Joe's stool and Kirk's and elbowed her way forward.

She paid no attention to either of them. Kirk threw her a dirty look but used the encroachment as a chance to sidle closer to the checkout girl, who giggled, revealing metal braces.

Didn't Mikey even pretend to card anymore?

The woman drummed her long, painted fingernails on the bar. Mikey pulled himself away from the hockey game.

"What'll it be?" he asked.

"I'll have a Yuengling."

Mikey met Joe's eyes and smirked.

"Good choice, darling. They're two for the price of one tonight, but what kind?"

She flushed. "Oh. Well, I just need one. Um . . ." She glanced over at Joe's glass, which somehow was already half-empty. "Give me what he's having. And, uh, why don't you give him my second one?"

Mikey gave her a close look but didn't say anything. When he'd left to get her drinks, Joe turned toward the woman.

"You didn't need to do that."

She took off her jacket and folded it over her arm, then leaned in toward him. He caught a glimpse of black lace and the swell of a breast under her tight purple sweater.

"I wanted to. I really don't need two—I'm driving. And you look like you could use another one."

"I do?"

"You do." She gestured toward his stool. "Mind if I hang my jacket over your seat?"

He jumped up. "I'm so sorry, where are my manners? Here, you sit."

"No, I'm fine. Really." She smiled.

"Please, I insist. After all, you bought me a drink. It's the least I can do."

He swept his arm toward the seat, and she ducked her head in thanks and slipped onto it in a fluid motion, made all the more impressive by her painted-on jeans and stiletto boots.

Once she was perched on the stool, she leaned toward him again, with another flash of skin and lace.

"Technically, I didn't buy you a drink. It's free, remember?"

A real smile spread across his face. The simple banter with a pretty girl was lifting his spirits. He suddenly felt much more charitable toward Kirk's penchant for reliving the glory days with every single female he could corner.

"I guess that's right. I'm Joe." He stuck out a hand.

She giggled and offered him her fingertips in return. Her hand was soft and warm. Her skin smelled vaguely like fruit, like the stuff they sold at the Bath & Body Works at the mall over past Firetown.

"Jen," she said.

"Nice to meet you, Jen."

"You too, Joe."

"You aren't from around here, are you?"

She shook her head, and her hair bounced off her shoulders. "No," she began, but stopped when Mikey arrived with the drinks.

She hefted the mug in her hand and said, "To Two-fer Tuesday."

He laughed and clinked glasses with her.

And they began to talk. It was easy and light, with none of the awkward pauses or stiff pick-up lines that usually attended a conversation between a strange man and woman in a bar, at least in his experience.

She seemed interested in hearing all about his furniture business, Rufus, even the defunct blues band he and Brent had started right out of college. She asked him a ton of questions and laughed whenever he said something mildly funny.

He managed not to mention Aroostine at all. And while he hadn't been attracted to Jen, so much as glad to have someone to talk to who didn't have a tail to wag, somewhere around his fifth beer, he felt something shift between them.

He thought she must have felt it, too, because she ducked her head and fiddled around with her shoulder bag—a nervous tic she'd been exhibiting off and on all night.

He smiled at her and tried to think of a way to tell her how he felt without sounding sleazy. It turned out he didn't need to form the words.

She put a warm hand on his forearm and leaned in close. Her breath tickled his neck, and she murmured, "What do you say we get out of here and go someplace more private?"

Arousal overwhelmed the sliver of guilt that had managed to pervade the alcohol, and he slipped a hand around her waist.

"Sounds like a plan."

His voice sounded slurred to his own ears, but she didn't seem to notice. She gathered her coat and bag while he closed out his tab.

He stumbled into the bar as he turned to leave, and Mikey eyeballed him hard.

"You sure you're okay to drive, Joe?" the bartender asked.

Jen waved off the question. "I'm gonna drive. He'll be fine."

She nestled her hip against his, and they walked out of the bar with their arms around each other. Joe was glad for it, because his legs felt awfully unsteady, and his vision was blurring.

He blinked, trying to clear his head, but everything was swimming. He was hot. Shaky. And so tired. The cold air hit his face as she hurried him across the highway, but still he felt dizzy, nauseous, and thickheaded.

He wanted to tell her he was sick—must have caught a stomach bug—but his tongue was too heavy to lift.

Then he was falling into the cab of her truck. She pushed him unceremoniously, dumping him inside.

His arms dangled loosely, and his head lolled back. He thought he must look like an ass, but he was too exhausted to care.

He closed his eyes and heard the engine roar to life. Then everything went dark and silent.

CHAPTER EIGHTEEN

Aroostine chewed the end of her Mirado Black Warrior pencil and considered her edits to Rosie's witness outline. The pencils were her lawyer magic. Every trial attorney she'd ever met had some pretrial superstition, and this was hers.

Not appreciably more expensive than the government-issued yellow No. 2s, her Black Warriors smelled like fresh cedar, wrote in thick, dark strokes, and, because they were perfectly round and smooth, rolled right off the table unless they were angled *just so.* They were the pencils she'd used ever since her first year of law school, when Joe had presented her with a finals care package of chocolates, tea, and the black pencils.

"They just reminded me of your glossy black hair and warrior spirit." He'd explained with a shrug when she'd held up the package of presharpened pencils with a quizzical look.

She used them. And she aced her first semester with a rock-solid 4.0 average. After that, she refused to use any other pencil. Throughout law school, studying for the bar exam, or her trial work back home, it was the Black Warriors or nothing. When she'd landed in DC, she'd been too timid to ask the taxpayers to fund her pencil obsession, but she'd found a stationery store in Dupont Circle that kept her in a constant supply of Black Warriors on her own dime.

An unexpected but happy extra benefit of her obsession was that writing her comments and critiques in pencil, rather than the standard red ink favored by senior attorneys the world over, seemed to soften the blow for the recipient of those comments. As Rosie put it, at least her drafts didn't look like they were bleeding when Aroostine handed them back to her.

As if she'd summoned her by thinking of her, Rosie eased the door open and poked her head in.

"I'm about to head into a meeting with the computer guys to finalize the exhibits for the expert's direct examination. Do you have any more notes for me on the witness outlines?"

Rosie's excitement at the prospect of going to trial was palpable, almost visible. Despite the fact that they'd been at it all day and the sun had long since slipped beneath the horizon, she seemed to shimmer with energy.

Aroostine hid a smile. She remembered that feeling of barely contained anticipation, although it had been a long time since trial preparation had held all the allure of Christmas morning for her. Even though this was her first trial at the Justice Department, she'd stood up in court dozens, maybe hundreds, of times. She suddenly felt world-weary. Old.

"Hang on, my comments are here somewhere."

She pawed through the pile of outlines on her desk and found her comments on the direct examination of the Mexican bureaucrat who'd been approached and offered the bribe. Jorge Cruz spoke impeccable English, and Rosie's Spanish was only marginally better than the little Aroostine could manage to recall from eighth grade with Señora Anderson. But when Aroostine had mentioned to Sid that she planned to let Rosie examine a minor witness or two, he'd surprised her by insisting Rosie take the lead on Mr. Cruz's testimony—testimony that was particularly crucial if the recordings were excluded from evidence.

Uncharacteristically, Sid hadn't explained his reasoning. He loved to explicate. At length. About everything. In light of his silence, Aroostine hoped his analysis went beyond the fact that the witness and lawyer shared a heritage. But the truth was, it was a plum assignment for Rosie, so neither she nor the junior lawyer was inclined to delve into the reasons.

A frown creased the younger woman's mouth, and a worried wrinkle crawled across her forehead as she scanned Aroostine's comments. Aroostine winced. Had she been too harsh?

She hadn't had much experience—or any, really—supervising junior attorneys when she'd landed at Justice. She'd borrowed a set of textbooks from some friends of the Higginses, whose daughter had majored in industrial management and had spent a weekend giving herself a crash course in how to manage and supervise personnel.

Had she forgotten to use a compliment sandwich? Or to phrase her suggestions as "I" statements?

"Everything okay?"

Rosie looked up from the page. She chewed her lip for a moment before answering.

"The edits? They're great. We're going to pulverize these idiots . . ." She trailed off.

"But?"

"But," she began, hesitantly, "can we talk about what's going on here?"

Aroostine pasted a neutral expression on her face and tightened her grip on the pencil. *She couldn't know about Joe. Could she?*

She forced the thought from her mind and cleared her throat. "What's going on?"

Rosie perched on the chair next to hers and leaned in. "You're in some kind of denial, right?"

The pencil snapped in Aroostine's hand. She dropped it to the table, her heart hammering. *How had Rosie found out about Joe?*

"Uh—"

Rosie rushed to continue. "I know it's not my place. This is your case, your trial. But, for goodness' sake, you nearly died."

Aroostine blinked.

"My surgical mishap? You want to talk about that?"

Rosie let out a short, frustrated huff of breath.

"Come on, Aroostine. First the court loses your filing. Then your apartment catches fire. *Then* the equipment malfunctions while you're in surgery. Does that really sound like a regular old string of bad luck to you. I mean, really?"

"Well, yeah. What else would it be? Do you think Womback and Sheely put a curse on me?"

She laughed at the image of the two sales representatives poking at a voodoo doll in her image.

"No, not a curse," Rosie said slowly, like she was speaking to a not-particularly-bright child. "But have you considered the possibility that these events may not be accidents? Or unrelated?"

"You think someone is doing these things to me intentionally?"

Rosie shrugged. "I don't know. I just think there are no coincidences. And all of this started to happen after we turned over the list of exhibits we intend to use at trial."

Aroostine cocked her head. "And?"

"And as soon as they got our exhibit list, the defendants filed a motion *in limine*."

"Now you sound like Sid. There's nothing remotely unusual about moving to exclude evidence. I mean, their attorneys do seem to take laziness to a new level, but they have to do something to earn their fee."

"Is it usual to only object to one proposed exhibit? Defense counsel finally stirred themselves to action, went through all the trouble of actually filing a motion, and only bothered to object to a single exhibit out of hundreds?"

Aroostine's pulse thrummed in her ear. When Rosie put it that way, she had to admit it certainly was *not* usual. In fact, it was highly *unusual.* So unusual as to be downright bizarre—a fact that she might have homed in on earlier, had she not been running as fast as she could on a treadmill of disaster and destruction. And now, divorce.

Rosie watched her face, waiting for an answer.

"No," she said slowly, "it's not typical."

"Right. It's almost like the defendants don't really care about winning the case."

"Okay, you lost me again."

Rosie pawed through the piles of documents stacked on the table and pulled out the exhibit list. "There's lots of stuff on here they could have objected to. Really, there's lots of stuff they *should* have objected to."

She passed the list to Aroostine, who flipped through it.

Rosie had a point. They had padded their list with dozens and dozens of exhibits that simply weren't admissible. It wasn't Aroostine's personal style to hit the other side with a document dump, but Sid had informed her in excruciating detail that the attorneys in his department strove to be over-inclusive, not selective. He'd given her his trademark sniff of exasperation and said, "It's not your job to decide what's in, Higgins. It's the judge's. Or do you think you're smarter than Judge Hernandez?"

"Okay. So?" she said now to Rosie.

"So. What they do care about—or at least what *someone* cares about—is making sure you don't stand up in court and mention those conversations for some other reason that has nothing to do with the FCPA charges. Mitch and I agree, it's the only explanation for everything that's happened to you."

"Mitch and you agree?"

She didn't know why she cared that Rosie and Mitchell had been talking about her string of bad luck, but she suddenly felt self-conscious.

Rosie arched an eyebrow at her, and she flushed.

Anyway, it wasn't the *only* explanation. For all she knew, her condo was built on her ancestors' burial ground. Or maybe Mercury was in retrograde. But she had to concede, if she was honest, that Rosie's suspicion didn't sound ridiculous against the totality of events.

The lawyers representing the named defendants, while on the lazy side, were widely viewed as ethical and upstanding. She doubted very much that they would be involved in anything shady.

Their clients, however, were criminals. Criminals, by definition, commit crimes. So while *she* might not be able to conceive of a reason to destroy federal court papers, commit arson, or attempt murder, there was no denying that a sizable population justified those very acts every day. If they didn't, the Department of Justice wouldn't exist.

She closed her eyes to think. Her very first case as a special prosecutor had involved a local politician who'd murdered a judge to prevent him from issuing an opinion that she'd mistakenly believed would hurt her business interests and a state attorney general who'd helped her in exchange for a slice of the pie. The politician's sister committed perjury multiple times to have her elderly patients declared incapacitated for her own financial gain. And that was in Nowhere, Pennsylvania, where the stakes were low, and the living was easy.

"What are you thinking?" Rosie asked.

"I'm thinking we need to pull a Woodward and Bernstein."

"Pardon?" Rosie threw her a blank look.

"*All the President's Men*? You know, Deep Throat? Watergate."

"Follow the money?"

"Follow the money."

CHAPTER NINETEEN

Joe's head was in a vise. It was being crushed. His mouth was sour; his tongue, lined with fur. He cracked one eye open, and the weak winter sun seared his eyeball. He squeezed his eye shut.

A jumble of memories from the night before swam through his headache on waves. The voicemail from Aroostine. The beers. The girl. More beers. The *girl.*

Her name was . . . Jen, maybe? Her hand on his thigh, warm through his jeans. The curve of her throat when she threw her head back to laugh. Walking out of the Hole in the Wall, hip bumping up against hip.

Where had they gone? What had they done?

He remembered the rush of cold air. Nausea rising in his throat. Stumbling into the cab of her truck. Then . . . nothing.

Could he really have blacked out? He'd never had a lost evening—not after drinking grain alcohol punch in the cornfield behind the high school, not in college, not when the band had played some crappy club that paid them in shots, not even after his bachelor party.

This was going to be one helluva hangover. His stomach cramped in agreement.

He sucked down the chilled air and breathed it out slowly.

Jen's bedroom was really cold. And her bed was unusually hard.

He eased his eyes open again and blinked against the onslaught of brightness and pain.

Jen's bed was no bed. He lay sprawled on a thin mat spread out on a bare wood floor. A scratchy wool blanket was tangled in a heap around his knees. He turned his head to the side and stared at the wood, forcing his dry eyes to focus on the grain.

He stretched out a hand and ran his fingers along a plank. Aged oak, four inches wide. His eyes traveled up to the walls. More old-growth oak. Hand-hewn logs. His woodworking brain fought through the fog and estimated them as having twenty-inch faces. The rafters were more of the same, with hand-hewn chestnut joists.

He was in an artfully restored log cabin. He'd place its original build date at 1800. Maybe a few years earlier. The coloring of the oak and the craftsmanship were slightly different from what he'd seen in old Pennsylvania barns and cabins. He pegged both as native to western Maryland. He'd bought similar boards from a dilapidated bank barn in Emmitsburg once.

Professional excitement overtook his queasiness. To a master carpenter, this place was like heaven.

He'd have to ask Jen about the cabin's provenance. Assuming she was here. The small room was still, and there was no evidence of a woman. There was no evidence that anyone used the room as a bedroom. Aside from the mat, it was empty. No dresser, no table, no lamps. Nothing.

There was a small square window carved high into one wall. It was bare. No curtain, no blinds. The adjacent wall contained a door. It was closed. He couldn't tell if it led outside or to another room.

He exhaled and pushed himself to standing. His legs shook beneath him, and sweat beaded his forehead from the effort of moving. He steadied himself and shuffled toward the door, trying to keep his head motionless.

He palmed the door. It was the same temperature as the rest of the room, so it couldn't be an exterior door. He ran a hand through his hair to smooth it down and tucked his shirt back into his pants, girding himself for the awkward morning-after conversation.

He pressed the curved, iron handle down and pushed outward. It was locked. From the other side.

His heart thumped.

He swallowed and tried to call out, but his voice was nothing but a croak.

He wet his lips. "Jen?" His voice was hoarse and husky but audible.

He listened hard. No response.

"Jen?"

His heart pounded even faster, and he dropped a hand to his back left pocket where he kept his wallet. *Empty.*

He forgot about the splitting pain in his head and swiveled around to look for his jacket, sweeping his eyes over each corner of the tiny room. *No jacket.*

On the other side of the door, he could hear shuffling and rustling. Someone was out there—someone who was ignoring his cries.

His dry throat closed. He grabbed the door handle and pulled, shaking from the futile effort. Then, as his stomach roiled with nausea and bile, he hammered his fists against the door, over and over, shouting a wordless, primal cry until his voice gave out and his hands ached.

Then he slumped against the wall and stared blankly at the slice of paradise that had just become his cell.

CHAPTER TWENTY

Aroostine sat motionless at her desk and listened to the sound of her wristwatch ticking and her own breathing. She'd sent Rosie off with instructions to run down SystemSource's corporate structure—an important and time-sensitive task—but her true motivation had been to achieve quiet and stillness.

If she was going to find some critical piece of information that she'd previously overlooked, she'd have to change her perspective. That was Tracking 101: you only see what you're looking for.

It had been one of her grandfather's first lessons. If you're focused on finding the squirrel, you won't register the bird. Or the edible berries hanging on the bush right in front of you. Or the slight depression in the earth where the last tracker had sat.

He taught her not only how to see, but how to use all her senses. First, he showed her how to examine a scene from all vantage points—crouching on the trail, lying flat on her belly, propped up on her elbows, hanging from a tree. Then, he wrapped a bandanna around her eyes as a blindfold and told her to listen to the same scene. She learned to hear the difference between a caw of hunger and a squawk of pain, between frozen ice thawing and water forcing its way through a chink in a dam. Next, she learned to smell the faint milky odor of a mammal nursing her newborns and the coppery scent of fresh blood to find a den or an injured animal. Her fingertips could tell if wood was dry enough to start a fire. She could taste whether wild berries were at their peak.

Most importantly, he taught her to be still and wait for an answer to reveal itself—a valuable skill in the wild, but not one she'd ever tried to transfer to her practice of law.

At this point, what did she have to lose?

She'd lived with the case file for weeks. She knew where the defendants ate breakfast, that Craig Womback preferred the aisle seat on airplanes, and that Martin Sheely always brought his kids gifts from the local street market or bazaar when he traveled. She knew who they reported to within SystemSource, that Womback had once had an affair with a secretary, and that Sheely always filed his travel expense reports the day after a trip. And she'd built a solid case against them for their attempts to bribe Señor Cruz. She'd mined the facts for every element she was required to prove, but that was all she'd looked for.

If Rosie's hunch was right, she'd obviously missed something that mattered a great deal to someone else. Time to stop searching for it and let it come to her.

She fiddled with the earbuds in her ears and hit "Play" on her audio player. Then she leaned back in her chair and listened to the recorded telephone conversations for what had to be the six hundredth time. This time, however, she would listen with no agenda, no purpose. Just listen.

Her pencil traced the words on the transcript as they filled her ears:

Mr. Womback: It's me. Can you talk?

Mr. Sheely: I have a few minutes. My flight's boarding now. How'd it go?

Mr. Womback: Time will tell. I met Cruz for drinks at some craphole authentic joint.

[Laughter]

Mr. Sheely: Did you talk dollars?

Mr. Womback: No. He's still skittish. You remember that dude in Poland, who freaked out when we brought up the specifics too soon?

Mr. Sheely: How could I forget? That was close. So, you're still dancing?

Mr. Womback: Still dancing, but I think he's game. He has the ultimate authority to choose the system; no sign-off required, so why wouldn't he pick ours and line his pockets at the same time?

Mr. Sheely: Let's hope so. We have to get this contract. I got yet another reminder from those pricks back at HQ.

Mr. Womback: [Snorts.] Let me guess—"Our investor has made it clear that his interest is in our international footprint. Government contracts are the most lucrative, stable way to expand that footprint"?

Mr. Sheely: They called you, too?

Mr. Womback: Frigging bean counters. They think it's so easy, let them pound the pavement trying to hit a sales quota month after month.

Mr. Sheely: You got that right. Screw them.

Mr. Womback: And screw that Ukrainian ballbuster, too.

Mr. Sheely: They're gonna close the doors. I gotta go.

Mr. Womback: Safe travels.

Mr. Sheely: Yeah. Adios.

[The phone call ends.]

She stared down at the paper and digested what she'd heard. The meat of the call was that the two sales reps had kindly hit every element she needed to prove a violation of the FCPA and had even named the Mexican official who was the target of the bribe.

But what else had they said? What was hidden in the call that someone wanted to keep buried?

Not the attempted bribe in Poland. SystemSource had admitted that as part of its settlement, and the Department of Justice had agreed not to pursue charges against the individual defendants for that conduct.

So, what?

The company was pressuring them to produce because an investor wanted to expand globally? As far as she knew, unless movies had lied to her, corporate greed was hardly unusual.

She nibbled her eraser and played back the recording in her mind. *The Ukrainian ballbuster* resonated. She circled the phrase on the transcript. Could it be a reference to another bribery attempt, one Justice hadn't managed to uncover?

No, the context made it seem like the Ukrainian was an insider, not a government official. Someone in the company's finance department? The investor?

Her cell phone vibrated on top of a pile of papers on her desk.

She ignored the buzzing. She imagined anyone who was texting her midday on a Wednesday was either her mother forwarding a picture of her floppy-haired guinea pig or her mobile carrier letting her know her bill was ready for payment. In either case, the text was less important than the task at hand.

She underlined the circled words. It was something. She'd ask Rosie to look for a Ukrainian entity in the web of companies that made up SystemSource.

There was a soft rap at the door. She looked up.

Mitchell leaned against the doorframe.

"So—are you Woodward or Bernstein?"

"As long as I don't end up like Archibald Cox, I'll be happy." She popped out the earbuds.

"Cox? The special prosecutor who Nixon had fired? Don't worry, I'm pretty sure Sid isn't going to fire you."

Of course he knew his political history. She bet his secret ambition was to someday be the solicitor general—or maybe even the attorney general.

"I'm not worried about me. Did you forget the other victims of Nixon's Saturday Night Massacre? His attorney general and the deputy AG both resigned rather than carry out the order to fire Cox. I don't need to drag you and Rosie down with me following some ill-advised hunch."

He shook his head. "There's something to this. Take a look at what Rosie's put together."

He crossed the room and handed her a printout. As she took it, his fingers brushed her wrist. Her pulse jumped at the contact, but she managed to keep her expression neutral.

She looked down at the diagram of interlocking companies Rosie'd managed to find so far.

"That's a lot of companies. Are you guys making any headway?"

She hadn't realized Rosie was going to enlist help, but she couldn't really fault her. They still had a massive amount of trial prep to get through. Every minute they spent playing investigative journalists was stolen from time that should have gone toward polishing their opening statement and nailing down the direct examinations of their witnesses.

He shrugged. "Maybe. I mean, we're finding lots of entities who could have an interest in the outcome of the trial or in preventing the tapes from becoming public. Too many."

Her eye trailed from the word *SystemSource* at the top of the page, along a series of vertical lines coming down from the word, branches on the company's family tree. It was a messy, overgrown tree. A jumble of subsidiaries, affiliates, joint ventures, divisions, and operating units spread around the globe, some connected horizontally, others branching off from a shared parent. A wholly owned Croatian subsidiary sat next to a co-owned Swiss affiliate.

Rosie had culled the names from the information statements that the company, as a publicly traded corporation, was required to file with the Securities and Exchange Commission. But those financial reports wouldn't tell the whole story; business lawyers drafted them with the express purpose of providing the minimum amount of detail needed to comply with the reporting regulations. This was a tree without fruit. And, somehow, the corporate structure had never been tied down during the initial investigation into SystemSource.

She felt a surge of irritation for the lawyer whose sloppiness had let that go undone, but she quickly dismissed it. The company had agreed to pay a big, juicy fine. What would have been the point of wasting taxpayer dollars on continuing to dig into its background?

Wow. You're really starting to sound like a government lawyer, she told herself with some measure of amusement. Aroostine Higgins, ladies and gentlemen, consummate bureaucrat.

She coughed to cover her giggle.

"What are the next steps?"

"I just wanted you to sign off on this list of entities. I have a friend who works at the SEC in the Division of Corporate Finance. We have a standing lunch date. Rosie's going to tag along and ask him to pull the files on all these interrelated companies. Want to join us?"

"Thanks, but I'll just grab a sandwich here. You know, you don't need to do that. We can get most of this stuff off EDGAR."

The Security and Exchange Commission's electronic database was public and freely searchable.

"Not all of it, though—only the information the registrants are required to report. Besides, it'll be quicker for him to do it. We'd have to run down each branch. He can just dig up the entire tree."

She frowned. He was right. But still. She didn't like the thought of him and Rosie running around calling in favors all over DC. She bit her lower lip but didn't say anything.

Mitchell looked at her closely.

"Why is it so hard for you to ask for help?"

She stared down at the desk for a moment. *Because I grew up a charity case. The only thing I want in life is to be able to take care of myself.* She swallowed the words and looked up.

He waited.

She shrugged. "You know, you don't have to help us with this. You have your own caseload."

She winced as her words hung in the air between them. She sounded ungrateful, petulant. That wasn't how she felt. Although she wasn't exactly sure how she *did* feel. Conflicted. Cared for. Grateful. Embarrassed.

A shadow of disappointment flitted across his face, and then it was gone. He leaned in close to her and tipped her chin back with warm fingers until she met his eyes.

"I'm not trying to help you win your case. I'm trying to help you stay alive." His voice was just above a whisper.

"Why?" she managed.

He stepped closer to her. For a crazy moment, she thought he was going to kiss her.

"I'd never forgive myself if anything happened to you."

He reached out and ran his fingertips along her cheekbone.

She tried to ignore the heat that flooded her body.

And then he stepped back. He watched her struggle for an answer. Then his mouth curved into a gentle smile.

"I better go. Rosie's probably waiting for me."

"Um. Okay."

Brilliant response, she told herself.

He headed for the door.

"Wait," she called. "Tell Rosie to look for a Ukrainian company, too. I don't even know if there is one, but . . . it's a hunch."

"Will do."

As he continued out into the hallway, she took a deep breath, then said, "Mitchell—I owe you one."

He turned and pierced her with an unreadable look.

"Don't worry. I'll collect." He flashed her another smile and left the room.

She watched him disappear down the hall and imagined what his lips would feel like pressed against hers. How his mouth would taste.

Stop that.

She jumped to her feet and searched the room for a distraction from the emotions she wasn't ready to admit she had. Her eyes fell on the iPhone. She scooped it up gratefully and unlocked the screen to check her text message. And every lustful thought of Mitchell was wiped from her mind in an instant.

She didn't recognize the sender's number, but she recognized the grainy picture. It was no guinea pig. It was Joe. He was stretched out on a dark floor. His eyes were closed. His mouth gaped open. The picture accompanied a terse, to-the-point message:

You have a choice: your husband or your case.

CHAPTER TWENTY-ONE

"I sent the message." Franklin's voice sounded dull and dead to his own ears, as heavy as the weight that had settled in the pit of his stomach when he'd seen the man's most recent text.

He'd just finished choking down an early lunch when his phone had dinged to announce the arrival of the picture of the man's newest captive along with instructions for Franklin to forward it to the lawyer with a very specific message.

He wondered if he'd go through the rest of his life cringing and tensing every time he heard the sound of a text arriving.

"Good."

Franklin hesitated. If the man wasn't going to bring up his mother, he had no choice but to push the issue. He inhaled deeply, squared his shoulders, and plunged ahead.

"Now, what about my mother?"

"She's resting comfortably."

The man delivered the news neutrally, like a hospital nurse reporting the condition of a post-op patient.

"That's not what I meant."

The man laughed.

Franklin's grip on the cell phone tightened, and he struggled to keep his emotions lidded.

"I know what you meant, Franklin. I told you. Change of plans. Momma's not ready to come home just yet. Besides, now she has a friend to keep her company."

Company. Franklin ignored the acid wash of guilt that hit his throat at the mention of Joe Jackman. He couldn't get hung up on the unavoidable fact that he was responsible for Jackman's current predicament. He hadn't had a choice.

"When, then? What more do you want from me?" he demanded.

"Don't whine. It's unbecoming. If the lawyer is smart, she will find a way to lose her case. Then, as I said in my message, her husband will be released—along with your mother."

"Lose the case? But the trial doesn't start until next week. You've had my mother since last Monday. She needs to come home. She's an old woman."

"She's fine." The man dismissed his pleas.

Franklin could tell by his tone that the man was getting ready to end the call.

"Wait—don't go. Please. What if Higgins *isn't* smart? What if she doesn't throw the case? What then?"

Silence.

Franklin asked the question knowing the man wouldn't say that he'd honor his promise and release his mother, but he had to ask anyway, because an impossible sliver of hope still existed somewhere inside him.

After a very long pause, the man said, "That will be regrettable for Mr. Jackman and your mother, then, won't it?"

Franklin pushed on. "What if she calls the police?"

The man exhaled loudly. "I suggest you see to it that she doesn't."

The soft click of the man ending the call sounded in his ear, and the remaining shard of hope he'd been carrying around shattered into a thousand pieces. He stared at the silent phone for a long moment, then chucked it at the wall.

His helplessness overwhelmed him, threatening to smother him.

There was nothing he could do—except hope that Aroostine Higgins stayed the course after she saw the picture of her husband.

CHAPTER TWENTY-TWO

The door groaned. Joe turned away from the small window. He didn't know how long he'd stood there, his forehead pressed against the cold pane of glass, staring out into the dense woods, hoping to see someone—a hiker, a hunter, anyone who could get him out of the cabin. But all he'd seen were two deer and a rabbit.

The quiet, empty woods outside the window had reminded him of Aroostine. And thinking about her made him feel almost worse than being locked in a log cabin. Almost.

The door opened inward, fast, and a tall figure stepped through the doorway and closed the door securely behind him. It was a man, tense and alert, ready for trouble, judging by his wide-legged stance and the raised shotgun he held.

Joe eyed him from his spot by the window. The shotgun was a smart choice, regardless of whether this guy was an accomplished marksman or a rank novice with a gun. And, judging by the stiff way he handled the shotgun, Joe guessed he was closer to the latter than the former. Not that it would matter: the shotgun would be easy to use and would easily hit a target, especially in a confined space like this one.

"Where's Jen?" he asked, keeping his voice casual.

The man shot him a quizzical look. Then understanding dawned on his lined face. He laughed—it was a guttural, harsh sound, completely at odds with his expensive haircut, cashmere sweater, black slacks, and highly polished, square-toed shoes.

"Jen? You mean the whore whose name you've been crying like a baby calling for his mother? I assume she's in some filthy trailer hunched over a computer, spending her fee. Virtual payment, who ever imagined," the man mused, talking more to himself than to Joe.

Whore? Jen was a prostitute. Embarrassment and self-disgust washed over Joe. He'd been targeted by a hooker. All she'd had to do was feign interest in his stories and engage in a modicum of flirting, and he'd walked right into a trap.

But why would anyone want to ensnare him? Master carpentry wasn't a field known for its cutthroat rivalry. And he was a go-along-to-get-along kind of guy. He just didn't have the sort of personality that would draw someone's ire—at least not so much that they'd go through the trouble of hiring a call girl to lure him to a remote wooded cabin to be held captive. Yet, here he was.

"Who are you?"

"This is not your concern."

Joe thought he heard the hint of an accent. Eastern European? Russian? He couldn't pinpoint it. But this guy clearly hadn't grown up in Pennsylvania.

He took a closer look at the man.

Late forties, maybe early fifties. Deep tan, with the attendant lines that habitual tanning caused. Short hair, brown, graying at the temples. He looked fit—tall and lean—but not obviously muscled. He could be a cycler or golfer, maybe a skier—some expensive sport for rich people. Everything about the man said "money." He looked out of place in the simple, rustic cabin.

In fact, he reminded Joe of many of his clients: wealthy New Yorkers who plunked down hundreds of thousands of dollars to renovate old farmhouses so they could have a country home to get away from their Manhattan lives.

This guy couldn't be some crazed Wall Street banker holding a grudge because his hand-crafted reclaimed wood bookcase had been delivered a few weeks late or some crap, could he?

Joe studied the man's face. No. He'd never seen this particular rich guy before.

The man looked back at him, impassive and patient. He showed no sign of worry that Joe might recognize him or be able to describe him later. Joe filed that scrap of worrisome information away for later consideration.

"Why am I here? That *is* my concern." Joe let a hint of steel edge his words.

The man raised a brow and seemed to consider his answer.

"All you need to know is that your wife needs to make the right decision."

"My wife?"

The mention of Aroostine stunned him, sending a wave of shock through his body.

"Yes, your wife. The lawyer. You do remember you have a wife, yes? I know you were quite eager to forget about her with the whore. But as I understand it, your divorce is not final. Aroostine Higgins is your wife. And she's still in love with you. That's lucky for you. It may save your life."

The rest of the man's words barely registered as Aroostine's name ran in a loop in Joe's mind: *Aroostine, Aroostine, Aroostine.*

He realized the man was waiting for him to say something. He cleared his throat and found his voice.

"Is she in trouble?"

The man smiled. "Your wife? No, Mr. Jackman, she's not the one in trouble. You are. Now, come. It's time for you to meet Mrs. Chang."

He covered Joe with the shotgun and reached behind him to open the door to the other room.

CHAPTER TWENTY-THREE

Aroostine splashed her face with water and patted it dry with one of the rough, unbleached paper towels from the dispenser. Then she gripped the edge of the vanity and stared at herself in the mirror. It would be obvious to anyone who so much as glanced at her that something was very wrong. Her face was pale, her pupils were dilated, and tension seeped from every pore.

Keep it together.

She exhaled and let go of the vanity. She dug around in her purse and found an old lipstick. She uncapped it and twisted the tube until the deep red nub of makeup rose above the rim. It had been banging around in her purse for ages, a freebie from the Clinique counter. Not her color. It would do.

She lined her lips then filled them in. Folded and kissed the paper towel to blot them, just like her mother had taught her. Then she employed another of one Mom Higgins's tricks: she rubbed her ring finger over the lipstick and dotted each of her cheeks red. Then used her fingertips to blend the color into her skin—instant vitality.

She examined the result. Progress. She no longer looked like a corpse.

She tossed the paper towel and gathered her resolve. It seemed clear to her that she had to continue to act as though everything was fine. At least until she could come up with a plan.

To do what? She had no idea.

But for now, her focus was on keeping her emotions in check.

She flashed her reflection an insincere smile and chucked the lipstick back into her bag.

Time to call her mother-in-law.

She pushed open the restroom door and strode resolutely down the hallway, extending her long legs and walking at a rapid clip, head upright, eyes ahead.

Her hands began to shake once she was back inside the safety of her office. She pushed the door closed and fumbled with her cell phone.

Dottie Jackman answered on the second ring.

Aroostine could picture her, sitting at the metal table in her kitchen, folding laundry, her attention fixated on the early evening news. She'd probably sighed deeply at the interruption by the ringing phone, but there was no hint of irritation in her voice.

"Jackman residence."

"Hi, Dottie. It's Aroostine."

She walked behind her desk and looked out the window down into the gray, cold Anacostia River snaking through the city, cutting off the have-nots from the influence, power, and money that pervaded their hometown.

"Aroostine! It's been ages!"

Dottie's extreme pleasure at hearing from her daughter-in-law answered one question. Joe hadn't mentioned the divorce to his parents. Well, she certainly wasn't going to break the news. Not now.

"How are you? And Chuck?"

She forced the niceties out through gritted teeth to keep from screaming that Joe had been abducted and was in danger and it was all her fault.

"Oh, you know Chuck. It's all of twenty degrees out, but he's out there in his workshop, tinkering away. Like father, like son."

"Speaking of Joe—"

"Yes?"

"I've been trying to get a hold of him, but I haven't been able to. Do you think you could pop over to his place and check on him? It's flu season, you know."

She knew Dottie knew. The woman was obsessed with influenza. She started talking about the coming year's predicted strain in September and didn't stop diagnosing everyone she encountered as a flu victim until sometime in April. Dottie would burst a blood vessel if Aroostine ever told her about the region's near-miss with H17N10.

"Don't I know it. Mary Elizabeth Murray was sneezing in the checkout line at the Shopping Kart last week. I'm thinking about getting some of those little paper masks to wear when I do my grocery shopping like they do in Asia. You should consider it, too, riding that subway system down there with all those people."

Dottie's voice grew breathless as her imagination geared up. Time to bring her back around.

"That's a great idea. Listen, about Joe, can you check on him?"

"Oh, honey, Joe's not sick. He's out of town."

"Where'd he go?"

"Well, that I don't know. But Chuck drove by and noticed Joe's truck at the Hole in the Wall early this morning. Now, you know, Joe's not one to go drinking in the day. Not like his great-uncle Pete. Lord, that man had a nip with his breakfast and just kept—"

"Joe was at the bar?"

Interrupting someone who was speaking was one of her biggest peeves. She thought it was rude beyond all imagination. But Joe had told her early in their relationship that knowing when to interrupt his mother wasn't a matter of being impolite, it was a matter of self-preservation. She'd resisted as long as she could, but after she'd been seated next to Dottie at a birthday party and had clocked one story about a chicken that laid eggs with double yolks at twenty-three minutes, forty seconds, she'd decided that a well-timed interruption here and there was an acceptable vice.

"No, no. The bartender told Chuck that he'd been in the night before, but he'd left with a . . . friend," Dottie explained.

She could tell from Dottie's hesitation that the friend had been of the female variety, but she didn't comment.

"So, he left his truck there and went out of town? That doesn't make any sense."

"Well, honey, I get the sense it was a sudden trip. Chuck went by the house to check on him. He wasn't there, but Rufus just went nuts when he saw Chuck. Poor fella was out of water and starving for food."

"Now, you know, Joe wouldn't go out of town without making arrangements for Rufus."

"Don't you worry about your dog, honey. We brought him back here. He's just fine. All curled up at my feet, snoring so loud I can barely hear what the weather guy is saying." Dottie chuckled.

"Oh, that's nice of you. Thanks, Dottie. I still don't understand how you know Joe's out of town. Did you call him?"

"Well, no. Turns out he left his cell phone at the house. Chuck noticed it on the charger. We were thinking maybe Joe decided to surprise you with a visit," Dottie offered, her voice tentative.

Aroostine was about to point out that Joe couldn't very well walk to DC, so leaving his car at the bar more or less ruled out an impromptu trip. The closest public transportation to Walnut Bottom was the bus depot fifty miles away. And she knew for an absolute fact that he wouldn't just leave Rufus behind.

Then it dawned on her. Dottie thought Joe was having an affair. She probably thought he'd left the bar with some floozy and had gone back to her place. Her mother-in-law was trying to spare her feelings about her husband's sleepover.

She felt her cheeks flush. But if Dottie wanted to pretend, she'd play along.

"Oh, maybe. That would be a nice surprise. It's been a while since I've seen him."

While she matched Dottie's pabulum with her own, her mind raced ahead: Joe had left the bar with a woman. Who was she? How was she involved in his kidnapping? Who could she get to help her find out?

Dottie babbled on about how much Joe and the rest of the Jackmans missed her and how they looked forward to her "temporary assignment" ending so she could come home. Left unsaid was the hope that her return would put an end to Joe's excursions with female friends.

She "hmmed" and "uh-huhed" her way through the rest of the conversation, only half-listening while she weighed her options. Calling the authorities was out until she had a better sense of who she was dealing with. She considered reaching out to Sasha—she had unofficial connections to agencies that didn't even officially exist—but she decided to keep that particular card in her pocket unless and until she needed to play it. For now, she'd handle this situation on her own.

She said her goodbyes to her mother-in-law and ended the call. Then she pulled up the text and stared hard at the picture of Joe while she braced herself for what would come next.

She punched in the cell phone number that had sent the text. Then she held her breath and listened to the ringing phone.

CHAPTER TWENTY-FOUR

Franklin blinked at the number flashing on the prepaid phone's display. The lawyer was calling him.

He wheeled around, panicky at the thought of talking to her.

Calm down.

He breathed out and reminded himself that he did know what to do. The man had given him a script to follow. He pawed through the papers on his kitchen table. He'd written it in his notebook.

Where was the notebook?

He had to hurry up and answer before she gave up and ended the call. But, he couldn't ad-lib. He had to find that notebook. He patted his pockets and felt the small rectangular lump in the breast pocket of his flannel shirt.

Relief flooded his body. He flipped open the notebook and thumbed to the page he wanted, then cleared his throat and answered the call.

"Hello." His voice cracked.

"This is Aroostine Higgins. To whom am I speaking?"

The lawyer sounded collected. Calm, somehow.

"Uh"—he consulted the notebook—"that's not your concern?"

There was a pause.

"Are you asking me or telling me? Because if that's a question, I'm pretty sure the identity of the person who's holding my husband hostage in an effort to interfere with a federal prosecution *is* my concern."

He grimaced. This wasn't going well. The man was going to be angry. Sweat beaded his brow, and he searched the notes, desperate to get this call on track.

"If you want to see your husband alive again, you know what you need to do."

"Actually, I don't know anything. That's why I'm calling you. What's this about?"

The man had told him to ignore her questions and stick to the words he'd dictated, so Franklin plowed ahead.

"Find a way to dismiss the charges against Craig Womback and Martin Sheely before the trial starts on Monday or your husband will suffer the consequences."

"What if I don't care?"

Franklin blinked and, in his surprise, deviated from his script. "You don't care if he kills your husband?"

"Actually, if you'd done your research, you'd know Joe and I are estranged."

He knew from listening to the phone message she'd left for her husband that she was bluffing, but her voice betrayed no trace of the lie. He skimmed the page for his next line, but she spoke again before he could find his spot.

"Who's he?"

"He?"

"You asked whether I didn't care if *he* killed Joe. So, that tells me you aren't the decision maker, which raises two questions. Who is he? And who are you?"

The room began to spin. His tongue was thick and heavy in his mouth. *Idiot.* Now he'd done it. The man was going to kill his mother because he'd screwed up. Sweat dripped into Franklin's eyes.

"Please," he blurted, all thought of his lines driven from his mind by desperate fear, "help me. He has my mother, too. He's going to kill her."

He was overcome by a combination of horror at what he'd said and relief at having finally said the words aloud. He began to sob softly.

He could feel the shock in the silence on the other end of the phone.

After a moment, she spoke.

"If what you say is true, I'll do everything I can to get your mother and my husband back, but you're going to have to tell me what's going on."

He considered what would happen to his mother, to her husband, and to him if she was wrong.

The man would kill them all.

And then Franklin surprised himself.

He sniffled, wiped the tears from his damp cheeks, and found his voice.

"I will," he promised.

CHAPTER TWENTY-FIVE

Mrs. Chang was in her late seventies or early eighties, Joe guessed. She looked frail and birdlike, with thin, hunched shoulders and close-cropped gray hair. Two of her fingers were wrapped and taped together with white athletic tape. She hugged her arms around herself, pulling her light cardigan tight against her body, and huddled near the woodburning stove in the corner of the room.

But she was uncowed.

When the man entered the room she raised her eyes and pierced him with a defiant, blazing gaze. Joe hurried to stand next to her, following the line the man traced with the shotgun.

The man's overly solicitous inquiries into how she was feeling and whether she was hungry went unanswered.

Joe didn't know who the old lady was, but he already liked her.

The man didn't react to her bold posture. Instead, he turned to Joe.

"She's not much of a conversationalist. But then I doubt you and the whore had a lot of scintillating discussions, either. Are you hungry?"

"Yes," Joe said immediately.

First, because it was true. Second, because he hoped it meant the man would go to a store to get food, giving him a chance to speak to the woman alone. As it turned out, the man had no intentions of staying.

"There are cans of soup in the cabinet. After I leave, make some for your new girlfriend too, and be sure she eats it. She needs to stay healthy." The man nodded to the far corner of the main room, which held a sink, a stove, and a small refrigerator. All circa 1960, by the looks of them.

Joe glanced at the kitchen area and then turned his attention back to the man, who was pulling on a black leather coat and supple driving gloves.

"You're leaving us here?"

"I have things to do. Don't bother trying to break the window or the door. She can tell you it's futile. And, if you do manage to get outside, there's nowhere to go. You're eighty-seven miles from a major highway as the crow flies."

The man zipped the jacket to his chin, then leveled the gun at his two captives in a fluid motion.

"Step back into the bedroom and close the door. If you come back out before I leave, I'm shooting you. Both of you. Now go."

The old woman glared at the man but obeyed the order. Joe trailed her into the room he'd just come from.

"Pull the door shut," she said in a soft voice. "He won't leave until you do."

Joe did as she instructed. A moment later, he heard the distant sound of metal thudding against wood.

The woman nodded at the sound.

"He padlocks it when he leaves. The window is padlocked, too, but it hardly matters. Too small to get through."

Her voice was gentle and sad.

"So, um, now what?"

"We can go back out to the front room and eat. When he comes back—probably not until tomorrow, he'll bang the butt of his shotgun on the front door and holler. We're supposed to come back here until he gets inside."

"Let me guess—or else he'll shoot us?"

"No flies on you. Well, come on. You said you're hungry; we might as well eat."

She opened the door and headed back into the main space.

"How long have you been here?"

She thought for a long moment, her eyes pinned to the ceiling as she tried to remember.

"This is the tenth day."

Joe whistled through his teeth.

"You're a tough old bird, aren't you?"

He hoped she wouldn't be offended.

She seemed to take it as a compliment, judging by the way her eyes crinkled.

"I've seen worse than that idiot."

He cocked his head, an invitation for her to go on.

"You ever hear of the Nanking Massacre?"

He had. "In December of 1937, the Japanese captured the Chinese capital of Nanking, beginning a six-week siege that resulted in the rape and murder of about three hundred thousand citizens."

She nodded her approval. "That's the one. Are you some kind of military history buff?"

"Something like that. My dad is. I watched a lot of the History Channel growing up."

"Well, I was two. My entire family was wiped out. Someone—I suppose I'll never know who—put me on a boat to San Francisco. And here I am. I survived that, I'll survive this."

His imagination didn't extend far enough to encompass being orphaned in a strange country at the age of two. Aroostine popped into his mind. Her background may have been less horrific, but it wasn't altogether different from the old lady's.

"I bet you will." He meant it.

"I'm more worried about Franklin."

Franklin? Joe swung his head around the small space. There was no way there was a third, unseen person in the tiny cabin.

Mrs. Chang shook her head. "He's not here. He's my son, back home."

Franklin had to be in his forties, Joe figured. Surely he could handle himself.

She seemed to read his mind.

"Franklin is what they call a change-of-life baby. Mr. Chang and I, God rest his soul, thought we couldn't have children. We made our peace with that. But the year I turned forty-five, God graced us with Franklin. He was an unexpected gift. And I'm afraid I raised him too soft. My husband died twenty years ago, when Franklin was thirteen. He's a bit of . . . a momma's boy."

She ducked her head in shame.

Joe obviously didn't know this Franklin character from Adam, but he felt compelled to comfort the woman.

"Come on, now. A kid with your DNA? He's got to have a steel core. Maybe it's just well hidden."

She met his eyes with a look of gratitude.

"I hope so, because he's mixed up in something serious."

"Why don't I fix us some soup while you tell me all about it?" He gestured toward the pine table and chairs jammed in the corner of the kitchen area.

She followed him across the room and arranged herself in the hard chair, then launched into her story while he banged around in the kitchen, looking for a ladle and a pot.

"Franklin's a very bright boy. He's good with computers. Coding and programming and things. But he's not good at life."

Joe turned a dirt-crusted knob on the stove, and one of the flat circles on its surface glowed to life. He stuck a cheap, lightweight pot on the burner and glanced over his shoulder at her. "No street smarts?"

"Exactly. He's naive. Like I said, soft."

A shadow of regret crossed her face, and he hurried to move on.

"What's he do? Does he have a job?"

She straightened in her chair, her posture suddenly full of maternal pride.

"He's very important. He works for SystemSource, writing their programs."

He opened a can of chicken stew and dumped it into the small, dented pot. He stirred it and tried to keep her talking.

"What do their programs do?"

She chuckled, a deep belly laugh.

"What *don't* they do? I don't understand the technology at all, but Franklin tells me they can monitor and control almost any computerized system from anywhere in the world. It sounds fantastical to me."

"What kind of systems?" He tried to keep his face neutral, even though it sounded creepy to him.

"Every kind of system." She held up the fingers of her good hand and started ticking them off as she recited them. "HVAC systems, security systems, medical equipment, elevators, sprinkler systems, traffic lights. You name it."

"Wow. That's something. What happened to your fingers?" He tried to make the segue sound casual. He suspected he already knew.

Her eyes darkened.

"Oh, that man wanted to teach Franklin a lesson. He didn't do something the man told him to do, so he snapped my fingers."

Rage swelled in his chest.

"Are you okay?"

She waved away his concern and responded with bravado. "Please. A minor irritation at worst."

He doubted that. No matter how tough she was, that had to have hurt.

"What didn't Franklin do? What does the man want him to do?"

She shook her head. "I'm not sure. It all has something to do with that woman lawyer."

"What woman lawyer?" he asked, freezing in place as he reached for two gray melamine bowls in the cabinet beside the stove. He already knew what she was going to say. He just didn't know why.

"Aroostine something or other. I've overheard him talking to Franklin. He wants her to throw some case."

CHAPTER TWENTY-SIX

Aroostine paced in a tight circle. The guy on the phone had said he'd meet her at the ice rink at the National Gallery of Art Sculpture Garden. The gallery and the gardens closed at five o'clock, so she loitered around outside the Constitution Avenue entrance to the skating rink and worried that he'd go to the Madison Drive entrance instead.

She pulled the glove from her right hand and swiped her finger across her phone to unlock the display. She redialed the last number she'd called and hurriedly jammed her cold fingers back into the glove.

The sun had set while she'd been on the Metro, and she'd emerged to find the temperature had fallen at least ten degrees. The chill didn't seem to be deterring the skating masses, though.

Groups of squealing, helmeted kids, some of them pushing chairs or clinging to the rails, circled around the rink. Serious enthusiasts weaved around them in graceful loops. And laughing, pink-cheeked lovers skated by hand in hand.

A memory flashed through her mind: Joe's hand, firm in a leather glove, gripping her own mittened hand, as he guided her unsteadily around the frozen lake behind what would later become their house. She was twenty-two and had never ice-skated in her life. His footing was sure; his voice amused and encouraging in her ear.

She blinked away tears and focused on listening to the ringing phone. *Keep it together.*

There was no answer and no option to leave a voicemail. The phone just continued to ring. At the same time, she heard an insistent ringtone over her shoulder.

She turned.

She didn't know how she expected the man to look. Tough. Enigmatic. Unkind, maybe. She certainly didn't expect what she found: a pale Asian man, his shoulders stooped and his back hunched as if he were trying to fold into himself and disappear. The man turned off his phone and shoved it into the pocket of his navy peacoat. He turned his collar up against the wind and ran his hand through his too-long hair, swiping his bangs out of his eyes and blinking nervously at her.

He was not fat, not thin. But he was soft, out of shape. A sedentary cubical dweller. Maybe a snacker, too.

She pushed down her nerves and smoothed her face into an expectant expression. This was his party.

He stared at her for a moment longer, then cleared his throat.

"Uh, hi," he managed to say.

She raised an eyebrow. "Hello."

Another throat-clearing noise. Then he gestured over his shoulder. "There's a cafe. Do you want to get some coffee?"

"Well, I don't want to ice-skate."

He half-chuckled and swallowed his laugh.

She hadn't been trying to be funny. She felt awkward meeting strangers—let alone strangers who were involved in her husband's abduction and were trying to convince her to violate her ethical obligations as an attorney. She'd just blurted out the first response that had popped into her mind.

He made a sweeping motion with his hand, as if to say "after you."

She headed for the entrance to the fenced-in sculpture garden and passed between two marble plinths that flanked the entrance to the garden. She was very conscious of the man following right behind her, so close on her heels that she could hear his choppy breathing, fast and shallow.

They entered the cafe and a burst of hot air enveloped her. She found a table near the windows and slung her bag over one of the chairs.

He unbuttoned his coat and blew into his hands.

"So, uh, can I get you a coffee?" he asked.

"I'll get my own drink. Thanks."

The awkwardness was excruciating—worse than a first date.

She dug out her wallet and walked up to the counter. He jogged along beside her.

"Hey. Hey, look at me."

She stopped and whirled to face him.

He coughed into his hand, then said, "I'm not a bad guy. I swear."

She stared hard at him. His shy eyes. The dark, deep circles that haunted them. His hunched, cowering posture.

He didn't *look* like a bad guy. He looked like a victim. A sudden swell of sympathy rose in her chest.

"I'm not saying you're a bad guy. I can just buy my own drink. Okay?"

"Okay."

He dropped her gaze and shuffled ahead.

Great. Sure. Feel sorry for this dude. Why not?

She reached the counter before he did.

"Can I help you?" the eager teenager asked, flashing her a bright white smile, a stark contrast to his dark skin.

"Yes. I'd like a medium hot chocolate."

"Oh, good choice! Whipped cream?"

"Of course." She smiled back at him despite her current miserable state. His bounciness was contagious. Before she realized what she was saying, she added, "And my friend will have a coffee."

The kid shifted his gaze to Franklin. "How do you take it, buddy?"

"Uh"—he blinked in surprise—"black, please."

"You got it. Just brewed a fresh pot."

The kids' fingers flew over the register keys.

Aroostine handed him a ten-dollar bill before Franklin could react. She shoved the change into the mug full of tips and was rewarded with another blinding smile.

He hurried off to get their drinks.

"Um, you didn't have to do that," Franklin mumbled. "But thanks."

She leveled a serious look at him.

"You're welcome. I'm going to assume, for this one occasion only, that you're acting in good faith and need my help. So, right now, you aren't a bad guy. But if you prove me wrong, there won't be a second chance. I'll be at the police station before you can blink."

Dad Higgins always said to assume the best of people but if they showed their true colors, believe them. It was a philosophy that squared with what her grandfather had told her when she was very young. People, like all animals, will reveal themselves if you give them a chance.

This was Franklin's chance.

Joe stared unblinkingly at the man. The man stared back.

Joe waited.

The man spoke first.

"Excuse me? Did you say 'No'? You refuse to do what I request?" His voice was cold. Emotionless. But Joe could hear the anger churning just beneath the surface.

"You heard me right."

The muscle in the man's cheek twitched.

"That is not advisable."

Joe shrugged and tried to ignore the almost paralyzing fear that gripped him.

"Says you."

"Mr. Jackman, this is not a game. You will set aside your pride and record the message as instructed."

"Or what?"

Joe had no intention of being filmed like some kind of hostage in the Middle East begging for his life. The man wanted him to convince Aroostine to tank her case to save him. He wasn't going to do it. Not because he was proud, but because he knew his wife. She wouldn't deliberately lose one of her cases, but she *would* do something dangerous and foolhardy in an attempt to help him.

The man's face darkened, and he narrowed his eyes. Then his mouth curved into a cruel, hard smile. He turned and strode into the bedroom, where Mrs. Chang somehow had managed to sleep through his unexpected, late-night return.

Sour bile rose in Joe's throat. He forced himself to keep breathing.

The man reappeared, dragging Mrs. Chang by her thin upper arm. She blinked, shielding her eyes from the sole lamp's light. Joe could see her trying to clear the disorienting cloud of sleep from her mind to figure out what was happening.

Unfortunately, Mrs. Chang, it's going to become clear all too soon, Joe thought.

The man drilled his eyes into Joe's.

"Now, then. Your question was what happens if you do not comply, is that right?"

Joe's throat closed.

Mrs. Chang's face filled with sudden understanding, but she didn't panic. She looked at Joe intently. He knew she was trying to send him a message not to cave into the man's demand.

But Joe knew the man wasn't bluffing. He would hurt Mrs. Chang. Again.

She stared harder and gave her head a tiny, almost imperceptible, shake. *Don't*, she mouthed soundlessly.

He shook his head at her, giving her an apologetic look, then wet his lips to tell the man he'd do it. He'd record the video message.

Before he could speak, the man laughed.

"How cute, this solidarity among my captives. She wants you to stay strong, Mr. Jackman. But you are not strong enough, are you? You do not have the stomach to watch me break her remaining fingers, one by one, until you do as you are told. You will acquiesce, yes?"

He forced out an answer. "Yes."

At the same moment, Mrs. Chang spat, "No. Whatever it is you want him to do, he's not doing it. You can go to hell."

In a swift motion, the man released her arm and backhanded her across the face. She staggered across the small room and landed in a crumpled heap against the wall.

Joe raced over to her. She looked up at him and gasped for breath.

"Don't do it. Don't do it, Joe," she whispered.

He bent and helped her to her feet.

"I'm sorry," he whispered back. "I have to."

She bent her head, and her disappointment in him radiated off her like waves. She shook her head sadly.

He patted her arm gently and turned to face the man.

"Let's get this over with."

Aroostine sat at the small, wrought iron table and studied the face of the man across from her. Franklin hadn't spoken since she warned him that she wouldn't hesitate to contact the authorities. He'd just stared at her owl-eyed for a moment and then trailed her to the table.

They sipped their drinks in silence for a moment. The faint strains of the music from the ice rink floated into the cafe and filled the space between them.

Finally, Franklin put down his coffee and dabbed his mouth with a paper napkin. "I am acting in good faith, I swear. But, please—what you said before? Please, don't even think of going to the police. He'll—he'll kill them."

His voice rose in a high-pitched panic.

The kid manning the counter looked over at them, his bored expression turning curious.

She smiled reassuringly at the kid and then turned to Franklin. "Shh. Calm down."

He gulped noisily and nodded. "Sorry. What are we going to do?" His voice quavered.

She considered the question for a moment, then exhaled slowly.

"First things first. Who are you? How are you tied up in this . . . this whatever it is? Let's start there."

"Okay, so, I'm a computer programmer. I, uh, did some hacking while I was in high school and college—nothing crazy, but I know my way through a lot of back doors."

"Back doors?"

"Right. A lot of times, a programmer will create a program for a client but leave himself a back door—a way in just in case he needs to fix or update something. Usually you'll hide it, so kids screwing around don't stumble on it and come in and muck things up. Follow?"

"I guess."

This might be more background than she needed, but she decided to let him go. He was clearly warming to his topic. He straightened up, leaned forward, and a glint of excitement shone in his eyes.

"So, I was hired right out of college as a programmer for SystemSource."

He paused to take a breath, but she jumped in.

"Wait—SystemSource, the company that makes the Remote-Control systems?"

He nodded. "That's the one. I know you sued us for trying to bribe foreign government officials. I didn't have anything to do with that."

"Okay," she said slowly.

Her brain was racing, signals careening around and bouncing off the walls like bumper cars, as she tried to make sense of the connection. It couldn't be a coincidence.

"I'll get back to the bribery thing in a minute, but stay with me, okay?"

As he got deeper into his story, his voice gathered force. Maybe she hadn't saddled herself with a bumbling wimp, after all.

"When I joined the company, they were selling systems software, but that was it. A client bought it, loaded it on their system, and used it to monitor things locally. I was given a project to update the software to make it more robust. I'm not really a software developer, so I left the basic program and started playing around, just kind of pretending I was a hacker. I had an idea, but I wasn't sure it would work. I worked on it here and there, whenever I could, in my free time for a couple of years."

"*You* developed the remote monitoring capabilities?"

She stared across the table, hot chocolate forgotten, at the unassuming man who had revolutionized the remote monitoring industry and, at least according to SystemSource's publicly filed financial reports, had rocketed the small company from a niche software provider to a billion-dollar player.

He beamed. "Yep." Then his face fell as he remembered the hell that singular achievement had thrust him into. "So, I modified the software so that it could be used to monitor and control almost any computerized system from anywhere with an Internet connection. My boss went nuts. I got a huge bonus and a promotion to lead the project. As you can imagine, clients loved it, and the software started flying off the virtual shelves. But then everyone needed to have it tweaked. Like, a security guard monitoring an apartment building is gonna need different capabilities from a building engineer trying to maintain a constant temperature and humidity."

"Sure," she said. What he said made sense, but an icy fist grabbed her chest. She had a feeling she knew where this story was headed, and it was nowhere good.

He plowed ahead, oblivious to her rising dread.

"Pushing out patches was labor intensive and time consuming. But for the first eighteen months, I just did it. I was working, I dunno, nineteen-hour days? They assigned me a bunch of interns, but I had to go over all their coding and check it because an error could be disastrous. I was drowning."

He stopped suddenly and stared out into the night, his gaze on the illuminated skating rink, but she knew he wasn't seeing it. He gnawed on his lower lip but didn't speak.

"So, I bet it seemed like a good idea to just go in through the back door you left yourself and tweak the software already in place, huh?" She was careful to keep her tone understanding. She didn't want to lose him now.

"It was. I get it, you know, clients don't want to think their systems are vulnerable. But this is safe. I'm the only one who can get in and modify them."

"But you can't be sure of that."

"I'm pretty sure. I hid my program in a security subkernel."

"Uh-huh," she said blankly.

"It's complicated, but imagine that there's a vault buried underground. That's where my program is. Users aren't going to stumble across it. And even a relatively sophisticated hacker who's looking for it isn't going to be able to find it." He grinned at his ingenuity.

"That was smart." Again, with the neutral tone.

"Thanks."

She hesitated. But she had to know, so she asked the question.

"Did you tell anyone at the company what you were doing?"

He ran a hand through his hair, a frustrated gesture. "Not exactly."

She waited.

"They didn't ask, and I didn't mention it. But there's no way my boss didn't know that something was up. I was being crushed by work and meeting all those deadlines—they didn't want to know."

Willful blindness. Plausible deniability. The hallmarks of corporate cowards the world over.

She nodded.

"And if they *didn't* know at first, they *had* to know after the VC infusion." His tone was fierce.

"VC infusion?"

"Right around the time that Womback and Sheely were screwing around trying to bribe Jorge Cruz, SystemSource was looking to spin off some subsidiaries. I'm not a business guy, but from what I understood, the company grew too big, too fast. It was a wild ride. The deal guys suggested selling off some units and maybe doing, uh, a reverse offering or something? Taking the company private again? I don't know the details."

"Okay," she said, filing the information away. She wasn't a transactional lawyer. She'd need someone to explain the details to her if they proved important. "And this VC thing . . . ?"

"Right. A venture capital company approached management."

"Venture capital? But SystemSource was already huge, and publicly traded at this point, right?"

She didn't know much, but she knew that venture capital companies specialized in helping start-ups grow. SystemSource would have been well past that stage.

"Right, but these guys came to us anyway. They offered an exorbitant amount of money for a tiny stake in the company."

She scrolled through her memory, trying to recall seeing any mention of such a deal in the SEC filings, but drew a blank. She made a mental note to ask Rosie.

"Do you know the venture capital firm's name?"

He shook his head. "No. But it wouldn't matter. The deal was structured through all these intermediaries to try to keep it sort of hush-hush. All I know is the sales people were probably under the same marching orders the programmers were under."

"Which were?"

"Don't mess anything up. We needed to show these investors that we were solid. Anybody who blew a deadline, missed a quota, went over budget—you were getting canned. No excuses."

"So, you think the sales reps tried to bribe Mexico because they were under pressure to produce?"

He shrugged. "Probably. Maybe? All I know is *I* was. I was back to around the clock even with my back door."

"Why?"

"The company set up a meeting between me and some suit who represented the VC guys."

"Suit? A lawyer?"

His eyes drifted to the ceiling as he tried to remember. "Maybe. I'm not sure. I wasn't sleeping much at that point, and, honestly, it's all a blur. I don't remember the guy's name, and I know I didn't get a card. Anyway, he wanted assurances that I could continue to customize the software if the sales volume continued to increase. I said, yeah, because I knew that was the right answer. And he pressed me for details: How could I be sure? What level of customer modification could I guarantee? How could I be sure?"

"What did you say?"

"He said the conversation was private. So, I told him. Not in detail. I was careful to explain that nobody else could get in through my back door, but that I could."

He stared at her, misery seeping from every pore.

Her throat felt tight and dry. "The venture capital group—or whoever this guy represented—knows that you, and only you, can get into all these systems?"

He nodded, tears shining in his brown eyes.

"And now they have my mom."

CHAPTER TWENTY-SEVEN

Aroostine raced down the stairs to the Metro station. Franklin's words echoed in her mind as she clattered down the metal steps, her scarf trailing behind her like tail feathers.

She jammed her card up against the reader and ran through the terminal to the platform for the Red Line, dodging an elderly couple and earning a dirty look from a lank-haired college student leaning against the column.

She didn't have time to care.

If Franklin was right—and the lump of lead lodged in her stomach told her he was—then Rosie was right, too: something important was hidden in her trial preparation materials. Something so important that someone was willing to resort to violence—and who knew what else—to keep it secret.

The Metro train rushed up to the platform and stopped with a disconcerting squeal of brakes. She elbowed her way to the doors of the closest car and waited for the passengers on the car to exit. A young couple struggled with an enormous stroller. One of the back wheels was stuck in the gap between the car and the platform.

On autopilot, she bent and helped the father raise the wheel, then stepped into the half-empty car with his thanks hanging in the air as the hydraulic doors whooshed shut behind her.

She flopped into the nearest seat and stared unseeingly at the public service announcement poster in front of her while she ran through what she'd learned from Franklin.

One, the business person—or lawyer or whoever he was—he'd met with on behalf of the venture capital group was not the same man who contacted him after his mother's disappearance. He was adamant on this point. He'd said the "suit" had been a typical white guy. No discernable accent or ethnic heritage. The man on the phone had the stilted speaking style and vocabulary of a nonnative speaker and a noticeable, but indeterminate, accent.

She unearthed a pencil and scrap of paper from her bag and scribbled, *Could accent be an act?* Then she resumed ticking off points on her mental checklist.

Two, Franklin's mother had been abducted after the defendants had filed the motion *in limine* in the FCPA case. The man knew Franklin could access court records. He grabbed Mrs. Chang to make sure Franklin followed his instructions.

She steadied the paper against the back of the seat in front of her and wrote furiously, recording the questions that flitted through her mind:

Why delete the opposition instead of waiting to see if the judge granted motion? Did something in opposition worry him—or was he worried about something in the defendants' motion? Can't ask defense counsel why they only objected to one exhibit—they won't discuss strategy. But why would they do that?

Overhead, a staticky, garbled voice announced the station. The train rocked to a stop. A thin woman who'd been dozing on the bench across from her jolted to wakefulness.

"Did he say Fort Totten?" she demanded in an urgent voice as she scrambled to her feet and edged toward the door.

Aroostine snapped into focus. "Uh, I really wasn't listening." She squinted at the words on the wall. "Yeah, it looks like this is your stop."

The woman nodded her thanks and rushed out the door.

Aroostine glanced at the map. Two more stops until her destination. She needed to pay a little more attention, or she'd end up missing her own station.

Three, the man was willing to kill. A shiver crept along her spine, and she hugged her coat tight around her body as if it were the cold and not that knowledge that caused her chill. But she couldn't ignore the evidence. Despite Franklin's protestations that he was careful, the facts were that someone could have died as a result of the fire; she could have died when he tampered with the equipment during her surgery; and both his mother and her husband's lives were entirely in the man's hands. The fact that, as far as they knew, he hadn't yet killed anyone seemed to give Franklin some measure of comfort. Not her. The unvarnished truth was they were dealing with a sociopath.

Be careful. He'll exploit any vulnerability he discovers. Rosie? Rufus? Mom and Dad Higgins? Mitchell?

She scratched out Mitchell's name and rolled her eyes at herself.

She glanced out the window to confirm the train was rolling into the stop before hers.

Four, to his credit, Franklin was being honest with her. He'd tripped over the words and she'd had to prod him a few times, but he'd copped to spying on her movements, listening to her calls, and telling the man about the message she'd left for Joe and how he'd tracked down Joe's personal information and shared it with the man, even though he'd known the man would use it against her.

She bit back her anger. It was hard to fault him. For all his brilliance with computers, he was a weak and naive person. He was trying to save his mother, by whatever means necessary.

He'd apologized over and over, begging her forgiveness. She'd told him they had to move on. But it was hard to let go of the hot rage in her belly. If anything happened to Joe—

Stop it!

She hadn't realized she'd spoken aloud, but she must have. The car's sole other occupant stood up and moved to the other end of the car in the time-honored Metro passenger's response to sharing space with the mentally imbalanced. He stood there watching her warily.

The train lurched to a stop.

She shoved the paper into her coat pocket, stood, and flashed the man, who was still eyeing her, a reassuring smile that she hoped exuded sanity and then exited the train.

She hurried through the station and out into the cold night.

Five, the man had no honor. Frankly, her short career as a prosecutor had already convinced her that honor among thieves was a myth. Most criminal conspiracies fell apart fast once one player was nabbed. Oaths of silence, gang loyalty, even the Mafia's omertà crumbled in the face of hard prison time. Criminals almost always acted in their own self-interest. Brother elbowed brother out of a drug territory, a wife skimmed off the top when she laundered her husband's books, a thief shot his boyhood friend and accomplice to increase his own cut of the pilfered goods. Whatever the crime, whoever the participants, everyone looked out for themselves. Why should this mystery man be any different, particularly when he had no real bond with Franklin?

No, it didn't surprise her in the least that the man had double-crossed Franklin. But Franklin was still outraged and bewildered that the man hadn't let his mother go as promised. The takeaway there, she mused, as she trotted across the street against the light, was that Franklin had *believed* the man would keep his word. The man, whoever he was, came across as someone of substance and some measure of integrity, at least according to Franklin.

She stopped in front of a gorgeous Dupont Circle mansion that had been carved into apartments, tucked the thought away, and took a deep breath before hitting the buzzer for apartment 302.

Before she could smooth her windblown hair out of her eyes, Mitchell's voice sounded through the speaker.

"Hello?"

She swallowed. "Mitch, it's Aroostine. I'm sorry to just show up like this. I . . . need your help."

There was a pause—not a long one, but not exactly a short one. She had time to regret what she'd done.

"Now, that wasn't so hard, asking for help, was it? Come on up."

The buzzer sounded and the door unlocked, saving her from formulating an answer.

As she walked through the vestibule she froze and wondered if Franklin was monitoring this building, too. She shook it off and started moving again. If he was watching, so be it. She had to trust him. Just as she had to involve Mitchell. She had no choice.

CHAPTER TWENTY-EIGHT

Franklin was beyond exhausted. He hadn't had a decent night's sleep since the night his mom disappeared. His stomach was sour and his brain was coated in fur, but anxiety and adrenaline had prevented him from resting. When he tried to sleep, his whirring mind took over, and his heart began to race.

Tonight, though, he could just *feel* that sleep was in his reach. Talking to Aroostine, enlisting her help, had eased his overloaded central nervous system. He'd returned home feeling almost hopeful. He didn't know what she planned to do, but she projected such a competent air that he believed she could somehow get him out of this mess. She reminded him of his mother—and if there was one word that described his mom, it was *capable*.

So when his dry eyes grew heavy, he turned out the lights, climbed into bed, and burrowed under his blankets.

The covers were warm and heavy. The room was quiet. His mind was still. He closed his eyes.

He was drifting between sleep and consciousness when the cell phone chirped to let him know he'd received a text. His brain rejected the sound.

Ignore it. Sleep.

He kept his eyes shut tight, but his pulse ticked up.

It's him. You can't make him wait. Remember what he did last time.

The pain in his mother's voice after the man had broken her fingers echoed in his ears. He opened his eyes and groped around his bedside table until his hand brushed up against the phone.

He pushed himself up to sitting and braced himself for the text message.

It was a video this time.

Please, God. Please let her be okay.

He was too afraid to hit "Play," terrified it would be a recording of his mother being tortured. He froze, his finger hovering over the arrow displayed on the screen.

I can't do it.

He reached over and flicked on the lamp, unable or unwilling to watch whatever it was in darkness.

Do it, already. Don't waste time, he ordered himself. He exhaled shakily and played the video.

And he began to tremble with relief. A shape appeared in frame, but it wasn't his mother. It was Joe Jackman. A ragged, pale Joe Jackman, staring sullenly into the camera.

For a second, defiance sparked in his eyes, so briefly, Franklin thought he'd imagined it. Jackman's expression flattened into resignation, and he began to speak tonelessly:

Aroostine, listen carefully. I am unharmed. You need to dismiss the charges in the case. You know which one. If you do, I will walk out of here alive. If you do not, I will not. The same applies to the woman. Please take this seriously.

Jackman finished reciting the lines and gave a baleful look to someone off camera. Then he glanced back and spoke directly to Franklin:

Your mother is fi—

The screen went black. Franklin sobbed. He could tell that Jackman had been ad-libbing at the end, and he prayed that the man hadn't made him, or Franklin's mom, pay for that bit of insubordination. At the same time, he was grateful beyond measure to know that, at least when the video had been made, his mom had been okay.

The phone sounded in his hand. Another text:

Forward to the lawyer.

Franklin began to shake again—this time, from fear. Forwarding this video to Aroostine might break her resolve. And if she decided not to go after the man, where would that leave him?

He walked out into the kitchen and flicked on the overhead lights. So much for sleep.

CHAPTER TWENTY-NINE

Mitchell put a kettle on for tea, while Aroostine marveled at the fact that he owned a teakettle and lived in this sleek, modern apartment. In stark contrast to the historic building that housed it, his place was all blond wood and geometric lines.

He peered out at her from the kitchen.

"Earl Grey or chamomile?"

"Chamomile would be great, thanks."

She warmed her hands over the hissing radiator while he rattled around in the cabinets, getting cups and saucers, spoons and sugar. He came into view holding a tray of cookies.

"Want one while the water heats?"

She shook her head.

"Double chocolate chunk," he wheedled. "And they're home-made." He pushed the tray toward her.

"You made them?"

"I'm a man of many talents."

She reached for a cookie. "Impressive."

"So, what's going on?"

He rested the tray on an end table and leaned forward with an expectant, serious expression.

She broke off a corner of the cookie and nibbled at it while she considered how much to tell him. She hadn't really planned this part. She knew she needed help. She didn't want to involve Rosie in a scheme that could prove to be career limiting. Mitchell had been around longer; he'd developed a reputation and a network. If this blew up in their faces, his career would survive. She hoped.

She abandoned the cookie and studied his face.

"Well, for one, I think you and Rosie are on the right track with the corporate structure stuff."

"How so?"

"Apparently, SystemSource received an infusion of cash from a private investment group right around the time that the Mexican bribery attempt took place. From what I understand, that transaction may not have been reported—I don't know the details, so it may not have been something they were required to report as a material change—but it was certainly material inside the company."

"Because of its size, you mean?"

He leaned forward, eager and excited, like a greyhound with a rabbit in its sights.

"Not exactly. It's more that the investors had a particular interest in one aspect of the company's business, and that put pressure on certain departments."

He twisted his mouth into a knot of exasperation. "Don't be coy."

"I'm not trying to be. It's just . . . I have someone inside the company helping me. I don't want that person to be exposed."

He seemed to bristle at the secrecy, sitting up straighter, but said, "Okay. Go on."

"The investors were most excited about SystemSource's ability to monitor and modify systems remotely."

"You mean the customer's ability to monitor and modify their systems remotely," he corrected her.

"No. I mean what I said."

She waited while comprehension filled his eyes.

"You mean—?"

"Yes. SystemSource's software contains a critical vulnerability. And I think the investor bought into the company specifically so he, or they, or whoever, could exploit it at will."

He blanched. She recognized the queasy expression on his face from her own reaction when Franklin had told her.

She forged ahead. "Somewhere, somehow, the FCPA case must expose that."

"Is it in the motion *in limine*?"

She nodded, impressed by how quickly he was piecing it together.

"I think so—either in the motion or our opposition. And I know what I have to do, but I can't involve Rosie. She's my direct subordinate, and it's too big a risk. But please don't feel like you have to do it, though, okay?"

He sighed. "Aroostine, I told you. I want to help you. What's the favor?"

"Okay, I swear it's not witness tampering, but what I need goes way beyond a favor into, um, possibly sanctionable conduct." She paused to let that statement sink in.

"Oh."

"Yeah."

He tilted his head and looked at a point over her shoulder for a moment, considering what she'd said.

Then he snapped his eyes back to hers. "Okay."

"Okay? Just like that—okay?"

He nodded and opened his mouth to speak but the shriek of the kettle releasing steam sounded from the kitchen.

"Hang on. I'll be right back."

She trailed him into the spotless galley kitchen and leaned against the refrigerator while he poured the water and fixed the tea. She watched his precise, economical movements and wondered if he could possibly be serious about taking the risk she was about to ask him to take.

He turned, balancing a saucer in each hand, and started when he saw her standing there.

"Oh, hey, here." He passed her a blue Fiestaware mug on an orange saucer.

"Thanks."

"Let's go sit." He nodded his head toward the living area and waited for her to lead the way back.

She returned to her spot on the sofa near the window. To her surprise, instead of taking the mid-century chair across from it, he sat next to her.

A sudden worry that his help might come with strings attached flitted into her mind.

"I'm married," she blurted. Her skin grew hot as soon as she said the words, and she knew her face was red.

His eyes widened and the lemon slice he'd been squeezing into his tea slipped out of his fingers.

"Oh? Well, you're just full of surprises tonight, aren't you?"

She set the saucer and mug carefully on the table and resisted the urge to hide her face in her hands. Instead, she straightened her spine and met his curious gaze.

"I guess so. While I'm sharing, here's another tidbit. I'm a member of the Lenape Nation. My parents drank themselves to early deaths, and my grandfather took care of me until he died when I was seven."

A sad shadow crossed his face, and she knew he was feeling sorry for a little Native American girl. She hurried on with the story.

"He was good friends with this white couple—the Higginses—who adopted me."

"I thought that was frowned on—taking a minority kid out of her own culture?"

She had neither the time nor the inclination to engage in a discourse about white aggression toward native culture or the fact that the Lenape Nation wasn't officially federally recognized—or that Pennsylvania *officially* had no Native Americans at all. It was all too complicated, politicized, and irrelevant to the issue at hand.

She shrugged off the question. "They were good parents. Anyway, they paid for me to go to this liberal arts college about thirty minutes away, and that's where I met Joe—my husband."

Mitch picked up his cup and sipped it but made no comment, so she pressed on.

"We got married the summer before I started law school. Joe was very supportive of my career"—she paused and cleared her throat before continuing—"up to a point."

He waited.

"When I interviewed for the position at Justice, he came with me to check out the city."

"But—?"

"I don't know what happened. He said he was on board with the move, but when it came time to actually pack his stuff up, he said maybe we should make sure I was going to like it here—you know, before he upended his entire life. To be fair, I wasn't at all sure I was cut out for the Department of Justice. I'd never lived in a big city before, and prosecuting federal crimes isn't exactly what I'd had in mind when I opened my little law office. So, we agreed I'd give the AUSA job a try, like a probationary period, and if it turned out to be something I really wanted, he'd make the move."

"And?"

"And it was, but he didn't. So, I've been living here, and he's been living back home."

She traced a circle around the saucer with one finger.

"So you're in a holding pattern? I don't see a wedding ring."

She laughed. "We were twenty-two and broke when we got married. I said I didn't need a symbol of ownership to prove anything."

A small grin creased his face. "Young love."

Her own grin faded. "A week ago, I probably would have said a holding pattern was a good way to describe the situation. But on Tuesday, I was served with divorce papers at work."

"This Tuesday? Like the day after your botched surgery?"

She nodded. "It's been a bad week."

"That's an understatement."

He started to reach for her shoulder, maybe to give her a sympathetic squeeze, but drew his hand back stiffly.

"And then it got worse."

"Now, that sounds impossible."

She swallowed around the lump in her throat and forced the words out. "Someone's been tracking me. He's using SystemSource's programs to remotely stalk me. I think it's the investor I told you about, or someone connected to the investor. He's behind everything that's happened lately. My missing filing, the fire, my dental surgery, all of it."

Mitchell let out a long, low whistle.

"Yeah. And he found out about Joe." She stared down at her lap and ignored the tears that began to fall. "And somehow, he managed to abduct him."

Mitchell's warm hand found hers.

"I believe you, but you realize how crazy this sounds, right? Are you sure?"

She extracted her hand, pulled her phone from her bag, and said, "He texted me a picture of . . ."

She stared down at the screen. The world froze in place. Her heart caught midbeat.

"Aroostine?"

His voice sounded distant, faint and garbled.

Her pulse was hammering in her ears like a trapped bird beating its wings.

"Sorry. I have a new text. It's from . . . him."

She knew it was from Franklin, actually, forwarding the man's instructions. But she didn't want to get sidetracked into a discussion of who Franklin was and how he fit into the picture—not with her heart thrumming in her ears so loudly it was making her dizzy.

He scooted closer to her on the couch and peered over her shoulder, his leg brushing against hers. This time, though, the contact had no effect. Her eyes were pinned to the video that began to play.

Dark half-circles shaded Joe's sunken eyes. Stubble on his chin and cheeks didn't quite hide the sallowness of his face. He looked spent and dirty. But not injured, she hurried to reassure herself.

He began to speak in a stilted, mechanical voice. He sounded like Joe imitating a robot.

"He's reading this," Mitchell whispered.

She nodded but didn't move her eyes from the video.

Joe's rage shimmered under the surface as he recited the man's demand that she throw the case. He finished his assigned lines and glanced away from the camera for a moment, then he looked back and said, "Your mother's fi—"

The video ended.

They sat in silence for a moment.

Mitchell exhaled shakily and spoke first.

"How's your mother mixed up in this?" he asked.

Aroostine closed her eyes briefly and considered her response.

Full disclosure, she decided. He had the right to know what he was getting into.

"Not my mother. Franklin Chang's mother."

Mitchell stood.

"I don't know who Franklin Chang is, but I know I'm going to need something stronger than herbal tea for the rest of this story."

As he walked toward the kitchen, he turned and shot her a look over his shoulder. "I'm thinking Scotch. Should I pour one or two?"

This response, she didn't need to consider.

"Two."

It was nearly midnight when she stood to leave, a little unsteady on her feet from the combination of booze, emotion, and exhaustion. He insisted on bundling up and walking her down to the street to wait for a cab.

They stood shoulder to shoulder in tired, drained silence and stared out into the gray half-light. She wondered if she'd ever get used to the lack of true darkness that attended the city at night.

After a minute, a Red Top cab cruised down the block slowly, probably circling Foggy Bottom's bars and restaurants in search of a fare going back to Arlington. Mitchell flagged it down, and the driver eased to a stop at the curb.

"Good night," she said as she slipped into the backseat, feeling awkward all over again.

He grabbed the door and held it open while she leaned forward to tell the driver her address. As she settled into the backrest, he leaned in and studied her face.

"I meant what I said. I'll help you. But you need to think this through. Are you sure you need to risk your entire career? If you want to go to the police, I'll go with you."

The cab driver turned his head to the side and stared studiously out toward the street as if he weren't listening.

She opened her mouth to respond, but Mitchell shook his head.

"Don't answer tonight. Sleep on it."

He shut the door softly and stepped back.

The cab driver returned his attention to the car and jerked it into drive. She raised her hand to wave goodbye to Mitchell. She saw the driver glance into the rearview mirror and size her up: Was she a fare who wanted to chitchat?

To forestall any small talk, she leaned back against the cracked vinyl headrest and shut her eyes. After a moment, the rhythmic motion of stopping and starting and the overheated interior of the car began to lull her into sleep.

She struggled not to doze and considered Mitchell's parting words. She had to try to help Joe and Mrs. Chang, even if meant the end of her brief prosecutorial career. But how? Her plan was still coming together but even once it gelled, she knew it would have a gaping hole: how to find them.

She needed to think. If she were at home, she'd clear her head by hiking up the trail to Alexander's Steeple, where she could lean against a two-hundred-year-old oak tree and do her thinking with a sweeping view of the valley below.

She opened her eyes and cleared her throat.

"Excuse me, sir?"

"It's Reggie."

"Change of plans, Reggie. I need you to drop me off at the entrance to Meridian Hill Park."

His eyes met hers in the mirror and flashed concern.

"You mean Malcolm X?"

"Um, the one between Fifteenth and Sixteenth. There's a drum circle there on Sundays?" She could have sworn it was called Meridian Hill.

He nodded. "That's the one. White folks call it Meridian Hill. But it'll always be Malcolm X to me."

"Uh, okay."

"Sister Angela proposed renaming it, oh, way back in the sixties. Didn't happen." He raised a hand and gestured toward the Black Panther fist sticker on his passenger side visor.

"You knew them? Malcolm X and Angela Davis?" She was momentarily distracted from her problems by the thought that she was being driven through DC by a piece of living history.

He grinned. "I did. That was a long, long time ago—a lifetime ago." The smile faded. "And I don't think that this is the best time to visit the park. It's late. And cold. Anybody you run into out there's gonna be looking for drugs—or worse."

"I'll be fine. I just need to clear my head."

"*You* aren't out looking to score, are you, girlie? Because I'm not getting in the middle of that."

"No. I don't use drugs. I just need a quiet place."

He squinted at her in the rearview mirror.

"I'm a country girl," she explained.

The city's rhythms and noise, its closeness and grime, had taken some getting used to, but she wasn't afraid of its residents. When she was just tiny, maybe four, her grandfather had taught her that no matter what environment she found herself in, she should respect the inhabitants, but not fear them. He'd pointed out a hive, buzzing with hardworking honeybees and said, "They won't hurt you, Little One, as long as you don't provoke them. To understand the bees, you must *be* the bee. To understand the bear, be the bear. But never fear another living creature."

He may have intended his counsel to be limited to wild animals, but she'd clung to it long after his death and had applied it each time she'd been thrust into a new environment: moving away from the Nation to live among white people, leaving the familiarity of the Higginses' home to go first to college and then to law school, and now here, in this strange, busy city that was home to the country's power brokers. She studied the people around her constantly, almost subconsciously. So far, it seemed to be working.

"Just the same," the cabbie interrupted her memory, "I'll wait while you do your thinking. Don't worry, I won't run the meter."

She didn't have the energy to argue with a geriatric Black Panther so she simply said, "That's very kind of you."

Then she leaned back and let her eyelids flip closed again for the rest of the short ride.

CHAPTER THIRTY

Joe couldn't sleep. He shifted on the hard floor and peered up at the window. In the distance he could make out a slice of the moon, three-quarters full and bright in the cold, clear night sky.

Somewhere out there, under that same moon, Aroostine had received the video by now.

Will she catch my message?

He traced a finger along a groove in the worn, scratched floorboards. He had been as subtle as he could so that the man wouldn't notice and had ad-libbed the line about Mrs. Chang mainly to distract the man from his movements. But had he been *too* discreet? Would Aroostine notice what he'd done?

He forced down the tide of icy panic that threatened to grip him. He'd tried. There was nothing more he could do.

As he turned onto his stomach, he consoled himself with one good thought. He knew Aroostine wouldn't turn against him simply because of the divorce papers, despite what he'd suggested to the man. She wouldn't let even justifiable anger or hurt stand in the way of helping him. It wasn't her way.

He remembered their first fight, during sophomore year of college. The details had faded with time but he remembered the accusations and anger that had flown around her tiny apartment, both of them inexperienced at working through relationship stuff. He'd stormed out.

After he'd had a chance to cool down, he'd shown up at her door with gas station roses and a greeting card, well trained by his high school girlfriends. She'd shaken her head in wonder and laughed, tossing aside the already wilted hothouse flowers. She led him outside to the rickety deck tacked on to the back of the apartment she was renting.

"You don't need to bring me cut flowers," she'd said, throwing her arms wide to encompass the starry sky. "There's a world full of flowers, trees, and stars."

"I just wanted to apologize," he'd explained, feeling faintly embarrassed and uncertain. Her equanimity had thrown him off balance.

"Then apologize, Joe. All I want is the truth that's inside you, not Hallmark's truth. Show me your truth."

He smiled at the memory, at the way he'd gathered her up in his arms. She'd wrapped her arms around his neck, and he'd carried her inside to show her the passion he felt in leisurely detail.

That was a long time ago. A small voice prickled in his head, dragging him out of his blissful past and back to his miserable present.

She'd left him, left their life together, to pursue her dream. She wasn't a twenty-year-old coed anymore. She was a high-powered federal prosecutor. Would she throw that away for him now?

He grabbed the thin pillow that Mrs. Chang had insisted on giving him and pressed it over his ears, as if that would drown out his own doubting voice.

All he could do now was wait. And pray. The rest was up to Aroostine.

CHAPTER THIRTY-ONE

Aroostine headed straight for the Buchanan Memorial, skirting the fountains, all turned off for the winter. She raced past the bronze statue of Joan of Arc, down the wide concrete aggregate steps, and through the corner of the park devoted to sculptures of poets. Guided as much by the bright moon and the faint stars as by the amber light filtering in from the street, she didn't slow her pace until she was directly in front of the statue of Law flanking the memorial to President Buchanan.

A lump of blankets stirred on a nearby bench.

"Park's closed, lady," a man said, peeking his head out from his warm cocoon to look at her.

"I won't be long," she assured him.

She turned to the classical sculpture. Its twin, depicting Diplomacy, stood sentinel on the other side of the memorial. She had no use for diplomacy at the moment.

She stared up at the statue.

The law.

It had meant so much to her for so long. It was an anchor that kept her from drifting into a well of uncertainty when she was learning to navigate the world away from her Native community. She loved the absolutes of the law.

But it couldn't supplant love.

She could live without being a lawyer; she couldn't live with Joe's death on her hands.

She exhaled. Her breath hung in a visible puff on the chilled air.

Her resolve strengthened, she pulled up the video of Joe's message to watch it one more time before returning to the warmth of the cab.

She stood perfectly still and stared at the screen. Joe's words burned themselves into her brain. And then she squinted. As he went off-script with his words for Franklin, he gestured oddly. In her dread and fear, she hadn't noticed the movements the first time.

What was he doing? He pointed, first toward the floor, and then out to the log walls.

She paused the video and her heart thumped in her chest, so loudly she thought it might wake the homeless man on the bench, who'd already forgotten about her and was snoring softly in his nest of blankets.

He's trying to tell me something? What? What is it, Joe?

She slowed her breathing in an effort to calm her racing pulse so she could think.

What would Joe want her to know? Where he was, so she could find him.

How could a wood floor and log walls help her find him? He was in a cabin. That didn't help.

And then she laughed and took off running toward the idling cab.

She hurried into the backseat and smiled at Reggie, who looked up from his sudoku puzzle in surprise at her noisy entrance.

"I'm so glad you waited! Can you take me to Hyattsville? You won't have to wait there." She was about to make herself an uninvited houseguest.

She pulled out the receipt from the cafe, where Franklin had scribbled his address and the number for his landline, practically begging her not to contact him any way but in person going forward. He was reasonably convinced that the man couldn't use his own program to monitor him, but why take the chance?

Reggie shook his head slowly as if to let her know he thought she was some kind of fool, but he tossed the puzzle book on the passenger seat and pulled out.

"Give me the address."

She read it off the scrap of paper and tried not to burst. The wood. Joe was telling her if she could identify the wood, she could find the cabin.

Up ahead, a green light turned yellow.

Hurry, hurry, she thought, willing Reggie to speed up and beat the light. But he slowed and then stopped as the amber glow turned red.

She tried not to groan.

She sat on her hands so that she wouldn't start surfing websites from her phone in her search for clues. If the man somehow learned that she was getting close, he might move his hostages. She jiggled her leg nervously.

The light turned, and the cab resumed its leisurely crawl up the mostly empty street.

Hurry.

"I'm gonna cut over to Georgia Avenue," Reggie said.

"Okay, that's great," she said, the words coming out fast.

He tilted his head and sought her eyes in the mirror.

"You sure you didn't score some speed in that park, girl?"

"Speed? No, I told you, I don't do drugs. I solved a problem. I mean, I think I did." She took a breath and slowed down to choose her words carefully. She didn't want to get him mixed up in her mess as a reward for his kindness. "I'm a lawyer. I have a big case coming up, and I think I just figured something out," she explained.

"Ah, inspiration. It strikes where it strikes." He said sagely and nodded, satisfied that she wasn't high.

A terrifying thought gripped her suddenly. What if the cab company used SystemSource to track its cabs?

She shook it off. So, what if they did? Only Franklin would be looking for her.

Right?

She distracted herself from unproductive worry by watching the moon through the cab's window. It wasn't quite full yet, but it would be soon. January. The Full Wolf Moon.

And a memory she'd long since forgotten came rushing back—a memory of the November night so many years ago when the Higginses came to get her from her grandfather's ramshackle cabin.

She'd been scared and sad, still mourning his death and anxious about leaving her home. She had answered Mrs. Higgins's solicitous questions in a meek voice, then leaned her head against the window of the station wagon and pretended to sleep.

But she'd peeked out from under her eyelids and had seen the moon—the Full Beaver Moon, as she knew it then—following the wood-paneled car. Her spirits had lifted. The moon, her moon, was coming with her.

And when the car had come to a stop, she'd squeezed her eyes shut, and Mr. Higgins had gently lifted her from the backseat and carried her into the house, where he placed her in a white-canopied bed covered with a pink and purple blanket and smoothed her hair over the pillow.

Her new parents stood over her bed looking down at her for a long moment, then crept quietly out of the room. After the door closed softly, she'd turned to look through the lace-curtained windows, and there it was. The Full Beaver Moon hanging low and ripe over a tree in what was now her backyard.

She was smiling to herself when she realized the cab had stopped.

"Are we here?"

"We're here."

She checked the numbers on the meter and removed double that amount from her wallet.

"Reggie, it was a pleasure to meet you," she said as she passed the money through the plastic window.

He counted the bills and sputtered in protest, "I can't—"

But she'd already pulled the door open and was making her way up Franklin's cracked sidewalk.

CHAPTER THIRTY-TWO

Thursday morning

Franklin groaned. The incessant beeping of his alarm clock cut through the cotton in his brain. He flung his arm out in the general direction of his nightstand and groped around until he silenced the noise.

He felt like crap. His mouth tasted sour and metallic. His dry eyes burned when he opened them and squinted into the daylight.

As he shuffled stiffly toward the kitchen to start the coffee, he cast a withering look toward the living room and the cause of his current sleep-deprived misery. Aroostine Higgins was sleeping in a tangle of blankets on the couch, having declined the offer of his mother's room, which truth be told, he'd made reluctantly.

She'd shown up at his door after midnight, just when he'd finally managed to calm down enough to sleep. She jabbered excitedly about native woods, then demanded to know if SystemSource could monitor his Internet use. Even half-asleep, he'd managed to explain that it was impossible for anyone at the company to use his own trick to spy on him without his knowing.

Satisfied, she'd commandeered his computer and had kept him up until dawn researching the different types of hardwoods native to the Northeast. By the time the sun was starting to rise, she'd compared several galleries of historic barns and cabins to screen-shots of the video of her husband and had determined the walls and floor of the log cabin where her husband and Franklin's mother were being held captive were made of old-growth white oak.

Franklin had vacillated between sharing her excitement and tamping down his own annoyance at this apparently academic exercise. Great, they were in a cabin that was at least two hundred years old and that had been constructed of hand-hewn white oak logs. So?

He hadn't had the nerve to question her, though. She'd been pumped full of adrenaline, so he'd just taken his cues from her—and had silently rejoiced when she'd finally crashed into a solid wall of exhaustion right around six thirty in the morning and col-lapsed in a heap on the couch. She fell asleep within seconds, and he stumbled back to his bedroom. His eyes closed as soon as his head hit his pillow.

But his sleep had been fitful and far too short. Two hours. He didn't even feel human.

He banged around in the kitchen, making no effort to minimize the noise as he started coffee and poured himself a bowl of cereal.

He checked the time and dialed the number to make his daily "I'm still too sick to come back to work" call. He'd learned that timing it for just before nine o'clock meant he could leave a mes-sage while his boss's secretary was busy mixing pounds of nondairy creamer into the swill that passed for coffee at the office.

He lowered his voice to an appropriate rasp and left the neces-sary update, making sure that everyone understood he was working from home, not simply lounging in bed.

"I need to do that, too," said a voice just over his shoulder.

He jumped, nearly dropping the phone into the sink, and turned to see Aroostine rubbing the sleep from her eyes. She'd pad-ded across the floor so quietly he hadn't heard her.

"Jeez. What are you—some kind of assassin? A ninja?"

She gave him a drowsy smile.

"No, a tracker. Did you think you're the only one?"

He smiled at that and felt his crankiness evaporating. After all, this woman was trying to *help* him. Help him get his mother back safely.

"Coffee?" he asked, gesturing to the hissing and steaming pot.

While Aroostine waited for Franklin's computer to come to life, she sipped her mug of dark roast and tried not to grimace. She wasn't a coffee drinker, but Franklin had no tea—or creamer, or sugar, or even milk. Apparently, mother and son both took their coffee black.

The bitter taste was outweighed by her need to clear the cobwebs of sleep from her brain. She took another hesitant sip and, for a moment, she thought of another black coffee drinker she knew. The temptation to call on Sasha McCandless for help was strong, but she simply couldn't continue to involve other people in this mess. She'd just have to handle it herself, with Franklin's help.

She sneaked a peek at him. With his hair sticking straight up from a night of restless sleep and clad in plaid flannel pajamas that she just *knew* his mother had picked out, he looked to be about twelve. Okay. Fine, she'd handle it all by herself with just a bit of help from Mitchell.

Franklin must have felt her eyes on him.

He turned and said, "Didn't you say you needed to call in to your office or something?"

"I e-mailed my assistant."

His eyes clouded.

"What?"

"What did your message say? Because, you know, I'm supposed to be reading your e-mail and telling *him* if there's anything noteworthy."

She tried to ignore the chill that tickled her spine at the casual way he talked about invading her privacy. "It was plain vanilla. I just said I'm too sick to come in and that I'll try to check in later."

"Aren't you supposed to be picking a jury tomorrow?"

She nodded.

"So shouldn't you be dragging yourself into the office even if you're sick as a dog?"

"Yes. That's the point. Everyone at work is probably having a fit right about now." She sent up a silent apology to Rosie, who would bear the brunt of Sid's outrage and would be scrambling to cover all the work herself, then she continued, "So you can tell the man that it looks like I'm cooperating. That sort of flaky behavior is consistent with someone who's planning to throw a case, don't you think?"

She waited patiently until comprehension lit his face.

"Oh, yeah, I guess it is. Great! Should I call him now?"

"Yes. But first—is there any way you can track *him*—even just to within fifty miles or so of his location?"

He shook his head and said in a mournful voice, "No. Believe me. I've tried. He's using a cheapo cell phone that doesn't hook into any of our systems. He's untrackable."

Aroostine set her mouth in a firm line. "No one's untrackable. Go ahead and make your call."

She turned back to the monitor, and her fingers flew over the keyboard. She'd find the forest that had been home to the white oak trees used to make the cabin's logs. Then she'd find the stream that the beaver kept showing her, although she had no intention of sharing the existence of her animal spirit guide with Franklin. And then she'd find the cabin.

What then?

She'd worry about that when the time came. And it was coming fast.

CHAPTER THIRTY-THREE

Franklin could hear his voice shaking. He paused and tried to steady it, so the man wouldn't think he was lying or holding anything back.

The man snapped, impatient and cold, "Are you there?"

"Yes. Sorry . . . I'm just . . ." He decided to go with a partial truth. "Well, I'm worried about my mother. And I haven't been sleeping and . . ."

"I do not care to hear your tale of woe," the man said in disgust. "Get to the point about the woman."

"Y-yes, of course," he stammered. "She sent an e-mail to her office. She's not going to work today."

"Did she say why?"

"She said she's too sick, but her calendar shows a full day of meetings to prepare for jury selection tomorrow and the case next week. It seems inconceivable that she wouldn't go to work, no matter how sick she might be."

He glanced nervously at Aroostine and was rewarded with a reassuring smile before she returned to whatever it was she was doing on his computer.

"Hmmm."

"I think this means she's going to do it. She's going to throw the case."

"Perhaps. You have had no response to the messages?"

Franklin exhaled and carefully recited the lines he and Aroostine had agreed on.

"No. I can tell they've been viewed. But she seems to have reacted by cutting off all contact with her friends and coworkers. She hasn't reached out to any of her coworkers, other than to send the message that she isn't coming in, and she's made no calls. I think she's in hiding."

The man was silent for so long that sweat beaded at Franklin's hairline.

At last the man said, "She may be. She is not staying at her apartment."

Franklin's heart pounded, and his chest constricted at the thought that the man might *know*.

This is it. You're going to die of cardiac arrest wearing plaid pajamas.

He struggled for a moment and then managed a shallow breath. "She's not?" he squeaked.

Aroostine's head swiveled in his direction at the panic in his voice. "No."

He braced himself against the counter with one hand and squeezed his eyes shut with terror. "Where is she?"

"I do not know. I have paid some of the front lobby personnel at her condominium building to keep me informed of her movements because the building does not use key cards that you can monitor. But, unlike your system, human intelligence is flawed and unreliable. She may have returned home and gathered her things unbeknownst to me. All that I know is she is not home now. My informant rang her apartment, and she did not answer. So he let himself in on the pretext of a potential leak coming from the unit above. Her unit is empty."

"Oh." Franklin searched for something to say while he imagined how Aroostine would react to the news of this latest violation. "Uh, interesting."

"Interesting? If you say so. Keep monitoring and let me know if she contacts anyone."

"Wait! What about my mother and, um, her husband? If she's going to do what you want, can't you let them go?"

The man snorted. "No."

Franklin waited, but the man didn't elaborate.

"But why not?"

An irritated sigh filled his ear.

Then the man huffed, "Because their presence will guarantee compliance. If she has set things in motion to cooperate, that is good. But they stay here until the judge declares . . . What's the word? A mistrial. Then I will uphold my end of the arrangement. Do not ask again, Franklin. It is becoming tiresome."

The words held a warning.

"Okay, I'm sorry. May I speak to my mother?"

"No."

The man ended the call, and Franklin turned to Aroostine, whose concerned eyes were still pinned on him.

"Um, he seems cautiously optimistic that you're going to throw the case."

"That's good. And . . . ?"

He plunged ahead, "And he has his claws in someone who works at your building. They're watching for you. You can't go home."

She raised an eyebrow and set her chin in a determined way but said nothing.

"Can I ask you a question?" he said.

"Go ahead."

"What's the effect of a mistrial? I mean, can't you just try these guys again?" He frowned in confusion.

"Yep."

"Then why—?"

"I have no idea what difference he thinks it'll make. I mean, he can't know this, but we probably won't refile the charges. These guys are small potatoes, and it'd be a waste of resources now that the case against the company is settled. But that's a political decision, not a legal issue."

"Unless he does know."

They stared at each other for a moment. He thought he saw her shiver.

"I don't even want to think about the possibility. Did he say anything else?"

"He's not going to release Joe and my mom until the trial is canceled or whatever."

"Of course he's not. They're his leverage."

She shook her head at his naïveté, and her black hair whirled around her face like a curtain.

He stood there for a moment feeling stupid and useless, then asked, "Well, now what?"

She tore a piece of paper from a legal pad and started scribbling a list with her chewed-up pencil. She handed it to him and said, "Can you read my handwriting?"

He scanned it.

Kitchen matches
Compass
Plastic poncho
Hand warmers
Small flashlight

Swiss army knife
Nuts
Thermos

"What is this?"

"It's a list."

"I *know* it's a list. So, I'm your errand boy, now? And you're going camping?"

She fixed him with a look.

"Do you really think I'm going camping?"

"No?" he ventured, not sure if he really wanted her to fill him in.

She seemed to sense his ambivalence.

"Listen, you want to see your mom again, right?"

He nodded.

"Then, don't ask any questions. Just do me a favor and get me this stuff. Pay cash."

"I know not to leave a trail." He tried but failed to keep the petulance out of his tone.

"Of course you do. Sorry. Listen, I know you probably don't think this is an important thing to do, but I really need this stuff and I can't risk being seen. Will you please go to the store and pick it up?"

He had the distinct feeling that he was being handled, but he didn't know what to do about it. So he simply agreed to the request.

"Okay."

"Thank you." She flashed a brilliant smile. "And while you're gone, I'm going to take a shower and borrow some more appropriate clothes, okay?"

She gestured toward the rumpled business suit she was wearing and the high heels she'd kicked off beside his couch.

"Uh, sure. Make yourself at home." He gave her the once-over. "You're at least eight inches taller than my mom, though. So I'll have to give you something of mine. Sweats?"

"Sweats, a base layer, anything you'd wear skiing would be perfect. Black is preferable. And I'm going to need some thick socks and waterproof boots."

He bit his tongue to keep from asking if she was planning to do anything illegal because he decided he really didn't want to know. Then he headed into his bedroom to find her some clothes.

CHAPTER THIRTY-FOUR

Joe and Mrs. Chang heard the man end his call and hurriedly abandoned their posts at the door to position themselves by the stove as he returned from the back bedroom. Their effort to eavesdrop had been futile, but it wasn't like they had a better way to pass the time.

The man banged into the room with a satisfied air. As always, he led with his shotgun. He noticed them huddling near the stove.

"Are you cold? Do not worry, soon you will be quite warm, quite warm indeed." He chuckled at some private joke and then nodded toward Joe.

"I am going out. Make yourselves lunch in my absence."

As he shrugged into his coat, Mrs. Chang cleared her throat.

"There's only two cans of soup left. Can you bring some more back?" she asked politely.

Joe had to admire how she'd maintained her dignity so far.

"Or maybe you could get a jar of peanut butter and a loaf of bread. You know, for a change of pace?" he suggested.

The man pierced him with an aggrieved look. "I do not take orders, Mr. Jackman. You will eat what I provide or you will not eat." He smiled charmlessly at the old woman. "Don't worry, Mrs.

Chang. If everything goes according to plan, tonight's dinner will be your last meal here. Now, get back there."

He waved them toward the bedroom with the shotgun.

Mrs. Chang crossed the room slowly, and Joe followed.

"Faster."

They increased their pace as ordered and closed the bedroom door behind them.

Joe waited until he heard the padlock bang against the outside door and the engine of the man's car rev to life.

Then he looked at his companion. Judging by her drawn expression and gray pallor, she'd had the same visceral reaction to the man's statements as he had.

But he shook off the feeling of imminent danger and said, "Sounds like we might be getting out of here soon."

She rewarded him with a withering look. "You're not an idiot, Joe. You know as well as I do, we'll never leave here alive."

Her words hung on the still air until he acknowledged them with a small nod of his head.

"We've seen his face. Heard his voice. We may not know what the heck is going on, but we know too much about him." He heard himself say the words in a flat, toneless voice.

"A-yup," she agreed.

They sat in silence for a moment.

Then, not knowing what else to do, he opened the door and walked back into the kitchen area.

"What'll it be? Minestrone?" He tossed the question over his shoulder with feigned cheerfulness but kept his eyes fixed on the mostly empty cabinet so she wouldn't see the despair that was eating at him.

"Oh, screw lunch. Get the whiskey."

The previous night, they'd found a dusty bottle of cheap whiskey lodged behind the pipe under the sink and had rationed themselves a shot each.

He considered protesting, but if they were right—and he knew in his bones they were—what was the point of pretense? He bent to retrieve the booze from its hiding place and plucked two mugs from the stack of clean dishes draining in the sink.

He poured them each a drink with a generous hand.

"Bottoms up," he said, passing her the first drink.

"Here's to a life well lived," she replied and clinked her stained porcelain mug against his.

He took a long swallow and waited for the burn to travel down his throat to his stomach. His eyes watered from the alcohol, or at least that's what he told himself.

"I'm glad to have met you, Mrs. Chang."

"Eunice. I think we can dispense with formality at this point."

"Eunice."

She tossed back a swallow and grimaced.

He cocked his head and watched as the weak winter sun streamed through the window and highlighted her face. A face that had seen horror and hope, feast and famine, and everything in between during her long life.

He blurted, "What's your biggest regret?"

Her eyes registered surprise and he started to apologize, but she cut him off with a wave of her hand.

"Please. We might as well have a real conversation in the time we have left."

She considered the question silently and then said, "Overprotecting Franklin. I love him so much, maybe too much. I tried to shield him from pain, from want, from difficulty. I don't think that's served him very well. And, for that, I'm sorry."

Sadness hooded her eyes.

His instinct was to reassure her that her son would be fine but he resisted the urge. She was right. There was no point in either of them pulling their punches now. So he simply nodded in understanding.

She cleared her throat. "And yours?"

He didn't have to think about his answer, but saying the words pained him—it felt like a knife being plunged into his gut. "Aroostine."

"Your wife?"

"Yeah. I don't know how to love her the way she needs to be loved."

Her eyes crinkled. "Go on."

"She has these dreams and ambitions that I know she wants me to support. But I just want to be with her. I don't want to live in a big city where she can have an important job with a fancy title. I just want her. Our dog. Our house. And I let that blind me to what *she* wants, I guess. I don't know. All I know is I made a mess of things. And then I asked her for a divorce in the most cowardly way possible. And I'll die in this cabin knowing I lost my wife because I wasn't brave enough to be honest with her."

She pretended not to notice the tears that fell from his eyes to the dusty floor.

They sat there in silence for several long moments, then she cleared her throat. "Well, I think another drink is in order. Don't you?"

He nodded numbly and poured the whiskey. He wished he had a piece of paper and a pen so he could at least write a note for Aroostine to try to explain what he'd done. The fact that he wouldn't have the chance to tell her himself was becoming increasingly real to him.

He raised his glass to Mrs. Chang and swallowed the drink in one gulp.

"We should come up with a plan to get out of here," he mumbled halfheartedly.

She didn't seem to hear him. She was staring at the inside of her mug. He supposed it didn't matter. His only real plan now was to dull the pain that threatened to tear him in half.

CHAPTER THIRTY-FIVE

Aroostine stood under Franklin's shower for a long time, letting the hot water stream over her body, and reviewed what she knew.

The cabin was somewhere in western Maryland, probably just outside Hagerstown, uphill from a stream. The woods would be remote, not a spot popular with hunters or fishing enthusiasts, and unlikely to be part of either the State or National Forest System.

She'd pulled up a map of the area and referenced the woods against the locations of all the white oak structures listed on the state's inventory of historic properties. She doubted anyone would be stupid enough to hold prisoners in a building that could be easily identified through public means, but she also knew from Joe that craftsman, and their materials, were decidedly local. That was particularly true more than two hundred years ago when travel was expensive and inconvenient.

So once she found a cluster of white oak structures near Hagerstown—in an unincorporated town called Long's Gap—she chose that as her starting point.

Then she'd gone through a list of nearby state parks and crossed those woods off on her map. That left three possible locations, two of which showed waterways cutting through them.

At that point, it was a coin toss. She chose the wooded area that was farther from town because that's where she'd hide captives, if she were the captive-hiding type. She'd start there, and if she didn't find the cabin, she'd hike to the other woods.

The lawyer part of her thought this was an abysmally deficient plan. The tracker part of her liked it just fine.

With great reluctance, she turned off the water, giving Franklin's hot water tank high marks for supplying steady hot water for the duration of her shower.

She wrapped one towel around her hair and used a second to dry herself. She held the towel tight around her body and crossed the short hall between the bathroom and Franklin's bedroom.

He'd left the clothes in a neat pile on the end of his bed. She pulled on the warm black pants and zip-necked sweater, surprised to see that they almost fit. The only other man's clothes she'd ever worn had belonged to Joe, and he was tall and broad-shouldered. As a result, his button-downs had hung almost to her knees, and she'd swum in his sweatshirts.

Stop thinking about Joe, she ordered herself as she wriggled her feet into the thick wool socks.

She padded in the direction of Franklin's mother's bathroom in search of a hair dryer. As she passed the kitchen, her phone chirped from its spot near the computer. She checked the display. Mitchell. She grabbed the phone.

"Hi," she answered.

"Hi? Hi, yourself. Aroostine, where are you?" Irritation seeped through the phone.

"I e-mailed and told Sid's secretary I was sick."

He lowered his voice and hissed, "I know what you told her. Everyone on the floor knows by now, the way Sid's thundering around."

"Oh."

"Yeah. So what are you really doing? Are you going to the police?"

"I don't know what you're talking about." She enunciated each word and kept her tone completely devoid of emotion, hoping he'd catch on.

Franklin had sworn that her phone calls were the only ones being monitored, and she believed that was true—as far as he knew. But it wasn't worth taking the risk to spell everything out for Mitch on the off chance that her adversary had redundant systems in place at the office. After all, he was paying someone to spy on her at her apartment building. Who knew what other eyes and ears he had in place?

"What? Oh . . . right. Never mind."

She rolled her eyes. She wasn't exactly a polished secret agent herself, but really. "Never mind" was the best he could do?

"Anyway, I really am sick. I was hoping you could help Rosie out in my absence."

"Sure," he said in a voice that was anything but sure.

"Just be there to answer her questions. She's never been to trial, you know."

"But, shouldn't you tell her—"

She cut him off before he could point out that she wouldn't actually be going to trial now either.

"Tell her I'll take care of everything else. She just needs to focus on the jury *voir dire*."

The federal *voir dire* process was usually a morning-long event where the attorneys asked questions of prospective jurors and tried their best to seat a panel of citizens who would find in their client's favor. Attorneys in private practice treated it as a critical part of the trial—maybe even the *most* critical part. After all, as her mentor used to say, if you seat twelve people who don't want to buy what you're selling, it hardly matters how good your case is.

Sid, and most of the prosecutors in his division, had a different view. They believed that they walked into the courtroom with the benefit of every doubt. After all, if you can't trust your government, who can you trust? Under this theory, every case was theirs to lose. Short of seating twelve anarchists or a foreperson who maintains that the post-Civil War government has been illegitimate all along, prosecutors almost always will encounter jurors who want to find in favor of the Department of Justice. As a result, *voir dire* preparation was nearly nonexistent in the Criminal Division.

The reality was that, in this particular case, it *didn't* matter, as they both knew, but she wanted to maintain the illusion that there would be a trial.

"*Voir dire*? Really?"

"Really. I happen to think it's crucial to the case."

"What about openings? Witness examinations? Don't you think it'll seem weird that no one's working on that stuff?" His frustration zinged through the phone.

"Just tell everyone I'm working from home and I said I've got it covered. Please help Rosie get ready for *voir dire* and tell her I said I'll meet her at the courthouse tomorrow."

There was a pause, but she knew he'd agree.

Finally, he did.

"Okay. But, what about . . . the other thing?"

"I'm working on that, too. It's under control. Just please don't forget what I need you to tell Rosie when she gets to work tomorrow morning. Everything hinges on that."

"Are you sure you don't want me to tell her tonight?"

"I'm positive. Just trust me, this will work."

Tomorrow morning, when it was too late for Rosie to do anything but comply, Mitch would tell her that Aroostine had already called in from the courthouse. He would tell her that Aroostine said to skip *voir dire* to draft an emergency motion for reconsideration asking Judge Hernandez to revisit his ruling to exclude the recordings. It would be a plausible request as far as Rosie was concerned, and it would guarantee that no one from the Department of Justice appeared in the courtroom when the jury selection was slated to begin. Aroostine was confident that, given the history of bad blood, Judge Hernandez would be enraged and act accordingly.

Mitch's voice was equal parts annoyed and concerned when he responded, "You know you don't have to do everything the hard way, right?"

Oh, but I do, she thought.

"I know. Trust me, you're going to be helping more than you can even imagine."

"If you say so."

"I do."

"Okay. Then, will you please at least do me a favor?"

"If I can."

"Please, whatever you're doing"—his voice broke—"be careful."

"I will. And thank you."

"For what?"

"For caring," she said, surprised to hear the words come out of her mouth. She hurried to hit the button that ended the call before he could respond.

CHAPTER THIRTY-SIX

Franklin took several deep breaths, readying himself for the confrontation ahead, then killed the ignition and stepped out of the car. He wrestled with the bags from the hardware store and the takeout containers from the Salvadoran joint. Out of hands, he leaned on the doorbell with his elbow and hoped Aroostine would answer.

He heard footsteps approaching along the hallway. A moment later, the door swung open.

As he hurried inside, he swiveled his head to make sure no one was watching from the Joneses' home, but their blinds were drawn.

"Something smells good," Aroostine remarked. She took one of the plastic bags from him and slammed the door shut all in one motion.

He engaged the deadbolt and then turned to face her.

"Pupusas. And empanadas."

"Pupusas *and* empanadas? Seems like overkill."

He shook his head and started toward the kitchen. "Salvadoran empanadas are totally different from Mexican ones. They're not savory; they're sweet. For dessert."

She started unpacking the food. "Even better. Were you able to get everything on the list?"

"Yep." He inhaled deeply and plunged ahead while she opened the cabinet to take out some dishes. "Two of everything."

"Two?"

"I'm coming with you." He tensed his jaw and prepared for an argument.

She looked at him for a long moment. He didn't blink.

Then she shrugged. "Okay. She's your mother. You should probably be there."

"Just like that?"

He couldn't believe she was just going to agree to let him tag along.

She reached into the silverware drawer for forks and knifes.

"Just like that." Then she smiled at him. "Also, I don't know how to drive, so I need a chauffeur. So, are we just going to smell this, or can we eat? Because it smells amazing. I'm ravenous."

She didn't wait for an answer. She carried her plate over to the table, pushed his laptop out of the way, and had a seat.

He followed her, still processing what she'd just said.

"You can't drive?"

"Nope."

"Why not?"

She shrugged and rested her fork on the side of her plate while she answered. "I don't know. I just never learned. Back home, I walked pretty much everywhere in town. If I had to get somewhere that wasn't walkable, Joe was happy to drive me. And there's no real need for a car in a city like this, right? You have the Metro system, buses, cabs. It's not a big deal."

"I guess not."

They ate in silence for several minutes. She was going to let him come with her. The nauseating fear and worry that had taken hold of him since his mother's disappearance faded and an unfamiliar feeling of anticipation gripped him.

Either his face gave him away or she read his mind, because Aroostine put down her fork and fixed him with a serious look.

"We need to be on the same page here. I need a driver, not a partner."

"But—"

She shook her head. "No. You're going to drop me off in the woods and then check into a motel."

"What? No," he protested. "I want to be there."

"I understand that. Believe me, I do. But it's better if you aren't with me—for a lot of reasons."

He dropped his voice to a whisper. "Are you going to kill him?"

She paused just a fraction of a second too long before she answered.

"Don't be ridiculous. Of course not. I'm a prosecutor, not an assassin."

He eyed her head-to-toe black ensemble pointedly but didn't press the point.

Instead he took a different tack. "It's not safe for you to be out there alone all night."

She threw back her head and laughed, a genuine, full-throated sound of amusement.

"Listen, you don't need to worry about me. I grew up in the woods."

"What, were you raised by wolves or something?"

"No. Indians."

Franklin felt his eyes widen but just nodded.

She went on. "I was born in my grandfather's cabin, in a small community made up of other members of the Eastern Lenape Nation. I lived there with my tribe until my grandfather died when I was seven. He was a master tracker. As soon as I could walk, he started teaching me how to track animals. I spent my first night alone in the woods when I was five. And trust me—it was way more remote than small-town Maryland."

"Oh. Wow."

"You didn't know? About my background?"

He shook his head. "No."

"That means *he* probably doesn't know either, right?"

"Everything he knows about you, he learned from me."

She smiled.

"Perfect."

CHAPTER THIRTY-SEVEN

Only if I have to.

As Franklin focused on the dark road, Aroostine replayed the uncensored thought that had gone through her mind when he'd asked if she planned to kill the man holding Joe hostage.

She'd never killed anyone. She'd hunted animals with a bow and a quiver of arrows, a lifetime ago, because that was how she and her grandfather got the food they ate. But after she moved into the Higginses' home, she never picked up her bow again.

She *had*, quite recently in fact, stabbed someone in the gut with a pair of scissors, but that was sort of a one-off situation where she was a guest at a destination-wedding that had been stormed by armed bandits. Did she really think she could kill another human being? She shivered at having to explore the darkest corners of her imagination.

Just be smart about things, and you won't ever have to find out, she told herself.

"So, let's go over this one more time," she said, more to distract herself than out of any desire to rehearse the plan, yet again, with Franklin. She'd walked him through everything twice before they'd left his house.

"Okay," he said, glancing away from the road long enough to throw her a quizzical look.

"You're going to drop me off in the woods and then circle back and check into the Wayside Motel."

"I'm going to pay cash for a room and use a fake name," he added dutifully.

"Right."

"Then I'm going to make sure my phone and laptop are fully charged. In the morning, I'm going to tap into the stenographer's feed and monitor the court proceedings."

"Yes. You'll be listening for the judge to get very irritated when no one from the Department of Justice shows up," she confirmed, ignoring the singsong note in his voice. She didn't care if he was annoyed. Practice and preparedness were her watchwords.

"And the other side will ask for a mistrial."

"Right. And because the judge hates my boss, he's going to grant the mistrial."

"And I'm going to contact the man and tell him about it."

"Right again."

"What if the judge doesn't? What if he reschedules the trial?"

She shook her head. "He won't. But if he does, just lie to the man. He won't have time to find out the truth."

"Because you're going to knock on the cabin door and say you kept your end of the bargain then politely ask for the release of your husband and my mother while I contact the local police and then let your friend Mitchell know what's going on."

"Something like that."

"Mmm-hmm. The end of this plan is a little . . . weak."

She shot him a dark look. "Do you have a better one?"

He fell silent for a moment.

"No, but I do have something for you."

"What is it?"

"You'll see."

He returned his attention to the road as they approached a sign welcoming them to Long's Gap. They passed a roadside vegetable stand, shuttered for the season, then a metal diner. A few moments later, a neon light announced the presence of a bar that made the Hole in the Wall look swank. Just beyond the bar, she saw a modern gas station, enormous and well lit, with cafe seating.

He checked the fuel gauge and turned on his blinker. He parked at a pump and hopped out to fill the tank. She eyed the surveillance camera mounted above the pump, then slumped low in her seat. She knew she was being paranoid, because the only person in the world who could hack the security system—if it were even hackable—was currently wrestling with the nozzle for the lowest grade gasoline. Nonetheless, she reached up and pulled the hood of her borrowed sweatshirt up over her head.

Franklin stamped his feet and breathed into his bare hands to warm them. She checked the temperature readout on his dashboard. It read 34 degrees. She rolled her eyes. He was *definitely* better suited to bunking down in a motel than roughing it with her in the woods.

He hurried back into the car, bringing a blast of bracing air with him. She turned to stare at him as he slammed the door.

"Did you just pay at the pump?"

He blinked at her.

"Relax, Aroostine, I used a prepaid Visa gift card that I bought at the hardware store—with cash."

She breathed out in relief, but then asked, "What's the point of that?"

"Even though he's not tracking us, there's no reason not to be cautious. Every time I hand over cash to a clerk, it's an opportunity for that person to remember me—or us. So I grabbed a card to use for gas and stuff."

She sat back, satisfied and surprised. He was proving to be a useful partner. What he did next upped his value even further.

"Excuse my reach." He leaned across the front seat and pulled open the glove compartment. He withdrew a small, black case and popped it open to reveal two earpieces and a set of cheap-looking cell phones.

He handed her one of each.

"What's this? I have a phone."

He powered on its mate before answering.

"Not like this, you don't."

She turned the phone in her palm, examining it. It looked like a perfectly ordinary phone.

"Okay?"

He bounced in his seat like an excited kid and angled his phone's display toward her.

"See, there's no guarantee that you'll have a signal way out in the woods, right?"

"I guess not. That's not good. What if *he* tries to reach you and you don't—"

He waved off that worry. "Realistically, I'll be reachable in the motel. If you're right, and he's nearby, *he* has cell service. But he's presumably not skulking around in the trees or whatever it is you plan to spend the night doing."

"So this phone will have service no matter what?"

"Not exactly."

She shifted in her seat and tried to mask her irritation. She didn't have time to play these games with Franklin.

"Then what's the point, exactly?"

"The point is I modified these phones to act as two-way radios that operate on a whole bunch of frequencies. I'm using the eXRS frequency-hopping spread spectrum so we should have a guaranteed communications range of several miles—at least five, probably more."

She had no idea what an eXRS frequency whatever-whatever was, but it sounded impressive. "Wow, you just did that today?"

"Sure. I had a bunch of old phones and some equipment just lying around the house. It was easy to play with." He shrugged with forced nonchalance, but his pride was palpable.

"Wow," she repeated, staring down at the hard plastic in her hand. "Great. And this frequency thingy is secure?"

"Pretty secure. Our communications will be less susceptible to interference or interception, but the important thing is that we'll be able to communicate regardless of mobile coverage. And, um, technically, we probably should have an FCC license to use these . . ." he trailed off.

Compliance with federal licensing requirements was quite possibly the least of her current worries.

"Whatever. How do they work?"

"Okay, so I made them voice activated. There's no touch-to-talk or anything. Just start talking and I'll hear you. We're fully charged, so you should be good until morning."

"And the earpiece?"

His face pinkened. "The earpieces aren't really necessary. I just thought they seemed cool—like for spies or something."

She swallowed her laugh.

"This is fantastic. I mean it."

He shrugged again and turned the key in the ignition. "It was seriously no problem. Child's play, really. We should get going, I guess."

CHAPTER THIRTY-EIGHT

Joe glanced at Mrs. Chang. She didn't look too steady on her feet, but most of a bottle of whiskey could have that effect. He felt a little bit on the wobbly side himself.

"You ready to eat, Eunice?" he asked as he opened the cabinet and retrieved the last two cans of soup. He turned them so she could see the labels. "Beef stew and minestrone. Pick your poison. Or do you wanna go out in style? I'll make both, and we can have a real feast for our last supper."

"Don't."

He cocked his head. Was the gallows humor upsetting her all of a sudden?

The boozy slur was gone from her voice. She crossed the room, tripping a little, and gripped him by the arm.

"Don't open the soup," she repeated.

He rested the cans on the counter and examined her lined face. "Why not?"

"Because we don't have to go to the slaughter like lambs, Joe." She stared back at him with a hard look.

"Mrs. Ch—Eunice, we've been over this. He has a shotgun. We have nothing." He swept his arms wide in a frustrated gesture to include the entire small space.

It was true. They'd spent hours scouring the cabin in search of *something—anything*—that would serve as a weapon, but the man had taken care to remove every blunt, sharp, or otherwise useful object; there were no knives in the silverware drawer, no scissors, no razors, no matches, and no hatchet, hammer, or wrench. The sole pot was a cheap, lightweight thing. There was no skillet. There wasn't even a can opener. The man provided them with soup that came in pop-top cans.

"We have soup," she answered.

He bit down hard on his lip. Even half in the bag, he'd been raised better than to call one of his elders a stupid cow, but he desperately wanted to.

Finally, when he was sure he could answer calmly, he said, "Exactly. We have soup."

He turned back to the counter, snagged the can of beef stew with his right hand, and reached for the pot with his left.

"No. Joe, we have *soup*." She grabbed the can from his hand and hefted it in her bony palm. "And we have socks."

She mimed dropping the can inside an invisible sock and winding it up to take a swing.

He stared dumbly at her for at least ten seconds. *Of course.* Any playground bully knew that a sock full of quarters made for a dangerously effective improvised weapon.

He flung himself into the rickety chair and started pulling off his black socks. His trembling fingers made it a harder task than it should have been. His heart thumped in his chest as he wrestled the socks off first one foot, then the other.

He jammed a can down deep into the toe of each sock, suddenly grateful for his oversized feet—or flippers, as Aroostine used to call them, teasing him—and then stood and twisted the leg material. He handed one to Mrs. Chang.

"Sorry about the smell. I've been wearing them awhile."

She waved away the apology and gave the sock a test swing.

"If memory serves," she began, "you'll want to hold this close to the heel, near the can to keep the weight stabilized."

He didn't ask what memory that would be, although the curiosity ate at him. There'd be time for that later—assuming this plan worked.

"So what's the plan?"

She blinked at him, surprised that he was looking to follow her lead. But she was the one who'd hit on the idea of using the cans. He assumed she had a plan.

He assumed right.

"Well, I was thinking that he usually comes in gun first, real fast, and shouts for us to get in the back room, right?"

"Sure."

"And he's always focused on you. He thinks you're the bigger threat."

He nodded. It was true—that was what the man seemed to think. Judging by Mrs. Chang's recent behavior, he suspected the man was wrong.

"When we hear him coming, I'll get behind the door. As soon as he steps into the room, you stop in the doorway of the back room but don't go in like we usually do. He'll have his eyes on you, and I'll crack him from behind. Then you can rush him from the front."

If he doesn't blow my head off first, Joe thought.

He saw the thought mirrored in her eyes, and uncertainty clouded her face.

He hurriedly said, "Let's do it. What's the worst that could happen?"

"He could kill us," she answered instantly.

"He's going to kill us anyway."

CHAPTER THIRTY-NINE

Aroostine patted the last of the twigs and dead leaves into place and rocked back on her haunches to admire her handiwork. She'd made better shelters, but this one would suffice for one night. It was located just one hundred paces north of the spot where she'd had Franklin drop her off, so finding her way back to their meeting point would theoretically be simple. It was situated due west of the stream she hoped would lead her to the cabin. And, considering how rusty her wilderness survival skills were, it wasn't half-bad.

She had dug out the vegetation from under a canopy of low-hanging boughs and insulated the ground with the leaf and twig debris. It was likely more comfortable than whatever cheap bodily-fluid-and-germ-encrusted mattress Franklin would be bunking down on at the motel.

She fiddled with the earpiece in her left ear.

"You there?"

They'd agreed not to use any names or other identifying information in their transmissions, both in case someone was monitoring the radio frequencies and because she had no idea how many laws they were breaking.

"Just checked in. This place is a dump."

She grinned at her makeshift bed, doubly satisfied with her efforts.

"It's just one night."

"Yeah. And I doubt my mom and Joe are enjoying even this much comfort."

The chagrin in his voice was palpable.

"Right. Listen, you're sure the man doesn't stay with them overnight?"

"I'm not positive, but I really doubt it. His usual pattern was to make my mom available to talk either in the evening or midday. I don't think he sleeps where he's holding them—he doesn't strike me as a roughing-it kind of guy."

"Okay. Good enough."

She checked the time. It was after two in the morning. If he wasn't sleeping there, he would definitely be gone by now. And if for some reason he *was* sleeping there, the overnight hours would be the best time to take the offensive against him. Tribal stories always featured surprise attacks under the cover of darkness that took advantage of the target's circadian cycle. First things first, though.

"What are you going to do now?"

"I'm going to take a short walk and then get some shut-eye."

"You're going to sleep?" His voice dripped with disbelief.

"Yes. Sleep is a weapon. I'm going to catch a short nap. I suggest you get some sleep, too."

She didn't particularly care what he thought of her plan. She knew her body and her mind, and she needed some rest.

"Okay, okay. Got it."

"Good night."

She looked up at the cloudless night sky to orient herself with the stars. The beauty of the low-hung moon made her catch her breath. It felt right to be in the woods again.

She scanned the ridge for animals or humans and saw nothing but the still, dark outline of vegetation and rock outcroppings. She paced a large circle around her campsite, mainly to reassure herself she wasn't sharing space with any predators. As she walked, she let the tension and anxiety drain from her body.

She wanted to fall asleep as soon as her head hit her pillow of dead leaves. Two or three hours would restore her. She always needed less sleep when she was outside, sleeping under the wide sky with no man-made light or noises to interrupt the world's nighttime rhythms. Joe once suggested she pitch a tent in the backyard and live there.

Joe.

She blinked the tears from her eyes. *I'm coming for you, Joe.*

Franklin shifted on the hard mattress and punched the stiff pillow into a concave shape with his fist. He flopped onto his side in a futile search for a marginally comfortable position.

How could Aroostine possibly be sleeping out in the woods, on the freezing ground?

He started counting backward from one hundred, but the hum of the motel's heating system buzzed so loudly he lost count. Through the thin wall, he heard a toilet flush in the room next door.

He pulled the pillow over his head, jamming it down over his ears.

Bright halogen lights painted his room in a slow arc as a vehicle pulled into the parking lot. So much for the room-darkening curtain.

A car door slammed, and laughing voices drifted across the lot.

He huffed. This was pointless. He was amped up on adrenaline and anticipation. Between his racing brain and the noisy motel, sleep was out of the question. He tossed the pillow aside and peered at the illuminated clock: *3:40 a.m.*

He reached over and switched on the bedside lamp bolted to the particleboard nightstand. Then, just in case Aroostine woke up and tried to reach him, he popped in his earpiece. After he'd gotten it into place, he fired up the laptop, and started surfing the Internet.

CHAPTER FORTY

Friday morning, before dawn

Aroostine stretched to her full length, then rose, brushing her blanket of debris from her clothes. The leaves and sticks had done their job. She was warm, dry, and rested.

She checked the illuminated face on the watch Franklin had provided. It was quarter to six. She'd slept longer than she'd intended.

She looked up at the dark sky and estimated she still had an hour and a half before sunrise.

She glided over the frozen earth, ghostlike and silent. Although her pulse was rushing in her ears, urging her to *hurry, hurry*, she forced herself to keep a slow, deliberate pace. She had plenty of time to find the cabin, and she knew if she simply paid attention to the forest surrounding her, it would reveal its secrets.

She walked due east, toward the stream she remembered from the maps. As she passed a copse of small trees, a flutter announced the departure of a bird. She squinted at the shape: it was a tufted titmouse.

The next sound she heard was the hushed whisper of water moving. She turned toward the noise. After a short while, it grew louder. She scrabbled up a small incline. As she crested it, she spotted the glint of the moon off the surface of a stream, *the* stream.

The stream cut through the woods, and she hewed to its curve, picking her way through the tall, brown grass drooping over the bank. Perfect cover for voles and mice as they raced through the forest for water, out of the sight of predators.

She followed the water around a bend and then stopped short, struck by a powerful wave of *déjà vu*. This was the spot from her vision. Just a foot away, the hulking gray boulder where the beaver had sat rose from the earth. She let her eyes travel down the hillside, across the water, and then through the tall trees up the hill on the opposite bank. She squinted and could just make out a dark square squatting among the dense trees. The cabin. A yellow point of light winked in the darkness.

Her breath came in shaky, shallow gasps. She'd had visions her entire life. Everyone in her family had visions. Once she'd gone to live with the Higginses, though, she'd worked hard to ignore them and push them down. In response, they'd grown opaque and hazy, more dreamlike than real.

But the beaver's visit in her bedroom back in DC had been crisp and true. Standing in the spot he'd shown her, she couldn't shake the feeling that she'd been there, *exactly there*, before—or the conviction that Joe and Mrs. Chang were just over the hill.

"You okay?"

Franklin's sleepy voice in her ear startled her.

"What? I'm fine."

"Okay, your breath got all choppy and stuff. Just checking."

"Why are you awake?"

"Couldn't sleep. I've been messing around online. I heard you rustling around a while ago."

"I think I found the cabin," she whispered

"Already?!"

He shouted so loudly she thought his voice would echo off the bank.

"Shh."

"Sorry. Wow. How'd you do that?"

She didn't have time to explain her animal spirit guide to a computer geek. "Ancient Indian secret," she deadpanned.

"What are you going to do now?"

"I'm going to check out the cabin."

"Now?"

"Yes. I want to see if I can get them out. Stay handy and be ready to call the police when I say."

"Why don't I just call now?"

"Let's make sure they're actually in there, first."

"Oh, right. Good point. Be careful."

"I will."

She stepped up onto the boulder and stared hard at the pin-prick of light.

Would she find Joe awake inside, waiting for her? Or something unspeakably bad? Or, perhaps worst of all, would she find absolutely nothing?

She forced herself to move off the rock and toward the water. As frightened as she was of what she might find in the cabin, there was no other way forward. She had to know.

She waded into the icy water and sloshed across to the bank.

CHAPTER FORTY-ONE

Joe started awake in the hard kitchen chair and blinked into the light.

"Wha?"

Mrs. Chang stood over him and peered down at his face, a worried frown creasing her lips. She was clutching her sock weapon with both hands.

"I hear something."

The urgency in her voice cleared the whiskey-coated cobwebs from his brain, and he sat up straight to listen, expecting to hear the low purr of the engine of the man's car or the crunching of footsteps over gravel. He heard neither.

He cocked his head. He thought he might detect a faint rustling or scratching against the wall near the window.

"That?"

She nodded, wide-eyed.

"It's probably just a tree branch," he soothed. He glanced out the window. "The sky's still gray. He won't come before sunrise."

The man had rarely come back to the cabin after he'd left for the night, but they'd agreed to sleep in shifts, just in case he deviated this time. They couldn't risk losing what might be their final chance to get the jump on him.

She shook her head. "No. It's not a branch. There's no wind."

"How can you tell?"

"No breeze around the window frame."

He reached down beside the chair and retrieved his sock from the floor, then pushed himself to his feet. The floor planks were cold under his bare feet.

He crossed the small space and entered the back room, trailed by Mrs. Chang. He pressed his free hand against the wall under the small window. She was right. There was no wind coming through.

He peered through the window out into the dense woods. A full moon hung on one side of the sky. On the other, the horizon was growing light. It was nearly daybreak. He saw nothing but trees.

He was about to turn to tell Mrs. Chang as much, when a spray of loose rocks hit the window. He jumped back and bumped into the old woman.

He leaned forward and squinted out into the night. A flashlight beam hit him square in the face, and he shielded his eyes.

"There's someone out there," he said, forcing the words out. His pulse was thumping so hard in his throat that it was almost impossible to speak.

"Oh, thank you, God!" Mrs. Chang murmured, sagging with relief.

"Well, let's not get ahead of ourselves," he cautioned, although his entire body was shaking with excitement.

He pressed his head against the window. The flashlight arced away and focused on the side of the house. Between the diffuse light and the moon, he could see an illuminated figure, tall and straight, covered in black from head to toe. He'd recognize that regal bearing anywhere.

Aroostine.

"Aroostine?" he shouted through the thick glass.

The shape bobbed its head. She mimicked tossing a ball or rock toward him and motioned for him to move away from the window.

He raised a hand, palm up, to stop her. "Don't. It's too small to get through. And it'll be too cold in here if you break it."

She nodded understanding and strained on her toes to see through the high, square window.

"Are you hurt?" she called.

"We're both fine." He spoke loudly, glancing beside him at Mrs. Chang, who was too short to see through the window.

Aroostine muttered something too low for him to make out. Then she yelled, "Tell Mrs. Chang she'll see her son soon."

Mrs. Chang burst into tears.

"How'd you find us? The wood?" he asked.

"The wood," she confirmed. "We can talk about it later. Mrs. Chang can't fit through that window?"

"Not a chance. It's way too small."

It was true. They had idly contemplated breaking the window, but it measured less than twelve inches square.

Aroostine looked up at him. Even in the dim light, he recognized the frustrated, determined way she held her jaw.

"There's got to be a way out. The only door is the one in front, with the padlock?"

"Yeah."

His adrenaline was draining away, chased by resignation and despair. He sneaked another glance at Mrs. Chang. Her shoulders slumped.

"Okay. Hang tight. I'll try to bust it open. If I can't, we'll call the police. I'm going to get you out of there."

She smiled her reassurance and turned to go.

He felt his heart crack open.

"Wait—"

She pivoted back toward the window.

The words he wanted to say were lodged in his throat. Beside him, Mrs. Chang jabbed him in the side with a bony elbow.

"Uh . . . thank you," he managed weakly.

Mrs. Chang *tsked*, and Aroostine's expectant face flashed disappointment. Then her smile returned, and she gave him a thumbs-up sign before jogging out of view.

CHAPTER FORTY-TWO

There was no way in. Aroostine banged pointlessly on the padlock with her flashlight, frustration screaming through her veins. Joe and Mrs. Chang were just feet away, and she couldn't get them out.

She caught her breath and said, "I can't get it open. Call the cops."

There was no response.

"Franklin?"

Nothing.

Her already-thumping heart went into overdrive. Where the hell was he?

"Franklin!"

"Sorry. I'm here."

"Is something wrong?"

"Uh . . ."

"What is it?"

"A black Mercedes just pulled into the lot. A man got out and started pounding on my door. I'm kind of surprised you didn't hear it."

So was she. She glanced down at the flashlight in her hand.

"Oh. I was doing some pounding of my own. So who's at your door?"

"It's *him*."

Her stomach dropped.

"Are you sure?"

"He just texted me. It says 'Open the door. You can't hide from me.' What do I do?" His voice shook.

She made sure hers was steady when she answered. "Listen to me. Do *not* let him in. Just barricade the door and call the police."

"Okay."

"Franklin, I mean it, no matter what he says—if he threatens your mom, whatever—do not open the door. Do you understand?"

"Yeah. It's a metal door. He can't get in, right?"

"Right," she hurried to assure him. "How'd he find you?"

Franklin's voice was thick with shame and anger. "I think he must have a tracking device on the phone he gave me. I checked it over and didn't see anything, though."

"Could be on your car," she offered. "It doesn't matter though, okay? Just hurry up and get the police out here before he gets here."

If the tracking device had been on the car, then the man would know where Franklin dropped her off. He might not know she was here, but he'd know that his secret spot had been compromised.

She ran around to the window to tell Joe and Mrs. Chang that their morning was about to get eventful.

⸻

Franklin wrapped his arms around his knees and rocked back and forth on the grimy bathroom floor. The cell phone the man had given him a lifetime ago sat on the tile, the text on its display searing itself into his brain:

Congratulations. You just sealed your mother's fate.

The man was still banging on the door to his room.

"Open this door, Franklin!"

The man's accented voice was hoarse from yelling, but his rage hadn't abated.

Franklin used the sink to pull himself to standing. He turned on the cold water full blast and splashed his face. Then he lifted the receiver to the phone affixed to the wall beside the light switch and tapped the digits 9-1-1 with shaking fingers.

As the phone rang, he craned his neck through the doorway and yelled toward the outside door. "I'm calling the police right now!"

The man stopped battering the door and let out a guttural roar. A moment later, Franklin heard the squeal of tires as the car sped from the lot.

He stared at the water swirling down the drain and started babbling as soon as the emergency operator answered the call. He seemed to have no control of the stream of words pouring from his mouth. He couldn't tell if he was coherent, but he just kept talking until the calm voice of the operator assured him she had all the information she needed. He let the phone fall, leaving it dangling by its spiral cord, and gripped the edge of the sink while he dredged up a prayer from the recesses of his memory.

Joe's pale, stricken face filled the window.

"He's coming!" Aroostine shouted. "He's not far away."

Joe's eyes flashed, and he hoisted a black sock into view.

"We're ready for him."

If she hadn't felt so desperate, she would have laughed at the absurdity.

"Is that a sock?"

He smacked it against his hand.

"It's what I have."

She held both palms up in a conciliatory gesture.

"Listen, just hang tight. Franklin's calling 9-1-1. They'll be here soon. It's almost over."

He stared at her silently for a moment then forced a grim smile. "Right."

She looked back at him, choking on so many things she wanted to say that she couldn't manage to say anything. Then the distant rumble of a car engine pierced the air.

Through the trees, she could make out a dark car snaking its way up the gravel road to the cabin. The man was here.

She turned and ran toward the woods, kicking up pebbles in her wake.

CHAPTER FORTY-THREE

Joe and Mrs. Chang were ready for the man when he burst through the door, his shotgun leveled and his eyes blazing with unconcealed rage.

"Get back," he demanded, gesturing toward Joe, who stood on the threshold of the back room with his hands behind his back. He waited for Joe to comply and didn't seem to notice Mrs. Chang was nowhere in sight.

Joe rooted himself to the floor and managed to keep his eyes on the man's face through inhuman effort. If he glanced toward Mrs. Chang's hiding spot she would be dead almost instantly.

The man glared at his defiance and took a menacing step forward.

Mrs. Chang stepped out from behind the door as it swung shut and wielded the sock like a sledgehammer. It glanced off the side of the man's head.

Whomp.

The blow sent him stumbling sideways. He roared in pain and surprise, then pivoted away from Joe and advanced toward Mrs. Chang with the business end of the gun pointing at her, blood gushing from his head.

Joe ran toward him. The sock was slippery in his hand, and the weight of the can pulled it sideways. He managed to connect with the man's head anyway, very near the spot Mrs. Chang had hit.

The man howled and fired a wild round into the wall.

Mrs. Chang threw herself to the ground and covered her head with her arms.

The man was wobbling, but he stayed on his feet.

He lifted the barrel of the gun and aimed it at Joe's head.

This is it.

Joe tensed and waited for the slug that would destroy his face and end his life. It never came.

Mrs. Chang dropped her sock and popped to her feet. She charged the man from an angle and forced the gun upward, pointing it toward the thick ceiling.

Joe pulled back and struck a third blow on the man's skull. This one connected solidly and reverberated through his hand.

Rivers of blood poured down the man's face. His hands slipped from the shotgun, and he crumpled to the ground.

Joe and Mrs. Chang stared at the shotgun as it fell. He felt himself tensing, waiting for a second blast. None came.

The gun rocked against the floor twice, and then was still.

Joe took his eyes off the weapon and saw the man crawling toward the door.

Mrs. Chang hurried toward the shotgun. Joe ran after the man.

As the man used the doorframe to pull himself up to standing, Joe grabbed his arm.

The man wheeled around to face him. Anger blazed in his unfocused eyes.

Without breaking his gaze, the man reached for the door. At the same moment his foot came up and kicked Joe squarely in the groin.

Joe gasped and lost his grip on the man's slick jacket as he doubled over.

The man opened the door and slipped out before Mrs. Chang could get a shot off.

She dropped the gun and joined Joe at the door.

He was focused on not sinking to the floor. The pain from the kick was radiating out from his groin in white-hot waves. Mrs. Chang grabbed his arm so he wouldn't fall.

The sound of the padlock swinging against the wood shook them into action. Joe forgot his pain.

They both tugged at the door handle.

The man was holding it closed from the other side as he fumbled with the lock.

"Harder!" Mrs. Chang cried.

They struggled to pull the heavy door open until a metallic thud confirmed it was no use.

"It's locked."

"We got so close," Mrs. Chang whispered in a defeated tone.

"Don't give up. Aroostine's out there. Franklin called the police. We're gonna get out of here."

He pushed back his own feelings of helplessness and found himself rubbing the old woman's arm and murmuring words of reassurance that he didn't quite believe.

She began to sob softly, her thin shoulders shaking.

CHAPTER FORTY-FOUR

Aroostine peered out from between the trees. Dawn had broken over the hill, and the morning light threatened to reveal her.

She tried hard not to think about the shotgun blast that had come from the cabin moments before the man staggered out woozily.

"Where are the police?" she hissed.

"I called them," Franklin said in her ear. "They're on their way. What's going on?"

"He went in. Joe and your mom had this plan to ambush him and run out, but it looks like it only worked partially."

"What do you mean?"

"They're still in the cabin. He's back out, but he looks pretty bad. He's unsteady on his feet, and he's covered in blood. Pretty sure it's all his," she whispered, even though she had no idea if it was true. She didn't mention the shot that had been fired.

If Franklin had heard it through the radio, he didn't bring it up.

"What's he doing?"

She squinted. He rested his forehead against the door and seemed to be holding it shut. She realized he was trying to lock his hostages back in.

"Crap. He's locking them in. I'm going to talk to him."

"What? No. Just wait for the cops now."

"I don't want him to leave."

He spluttered something, but she tuned out the noise and stepped out from behind the trees.

The man slapped a hand against the door, then stumbled toward his car but, so far, she hadn't heard the roar of an engine springing to life.

She started along the gravel path.

A car trunk thumped shut.

She stepped into the path, blocking the route to the cabin and planted her feet solidly.

The man came back into view, lugging something heavy, judging by the way whatever it was bumped against his thigh. She narrowed her eyes for a closer look. It was a plastic gallon container. The kind a person would keep in the trunk of a car to fill in case he ran out of gas.

"Oh, no. No."

Her mind flashed back to the piles of dead leaves and twigs that had ringed the house. She hadn't given them a second thought when she was trying to get into the house.

Kindling.

"What?"

She ignored the question as the man caught sight of her and stopped short.

He stared at her in disbelief through a curtain of blood.

"You." The word came out thickly.

He was in bad shape. He appeared to be bleeding from several spots on his head, but all she could focus on was the container in his hands. She could hear the liquid sloshing inside as he fumbled with the cap.

"Yes, it's me," she said. Her voice was calm and smooth despite the fear churning in her mind. "As you can see, I won't be in court today. The judge will declare a mistrial, just like you wanted. I kept my end of the bargain. Now you're going to keep yours, right?"

He wiped his face with his free hand and spat on the ground at her feet. Then he chuckled. "No."

He advanced toward her, continuing to uncap the container as he walked.

"Listen. I don't care about the trial. I really don't. Just, please, unlock the door and let Joe and Mrs. Chang walk away from here. You don't want two deaths on your hands."

"Two? I think you miscount. The number will be three," he said as he lifted the container and swung it in an arc.

A wave of gasoline splashed over her, running into her eyes and mouth. She gasped and retched. By the time her vision cleared, he'd already struck a long wooden match.

"I suggest you step aside," he said through clenched teeth.

He jabbed the match toward her, and its flame danced in the air.

She hesitated.

He threw the match at her feet, where the gasoline dripping off her had already begun to pool, and fire rose from the ground.

He raised a second match. She jogged backward, afraid to turn her back on him, until she reached the bushes that led into the woods, then turned and sprinted toward the stream.

She waded out to the middle and submerged her head in the icy water without stopping to think about the effect it might have on the radio or the earpiece. Her only thought was to get the taste of gasoline out of her mouth and wash the fuel off her body.

She dragged herself out of the stream, her wet clothes hanging heavily, and trudged back up the hill.

The cabin was already surrounded by a ring of flames when she reached the top of the hill. The black car was gone.

"He started a fire. The cabin's on fire!" she barked into the earpiece

There was no response. She had no idea if the radio was working or if Franklin could hear her.

"Franklin?"

No response.

The phone tugged at her waterlogged clothes and slowed her down. She pulled the earpiece from her ear and tossed the unit aside.

Flames leaped hypnotically, ringing the cabin. The heaps of dry wood and densely packed leaf debris the man had placed around the small structure were ablaze and burning quickly. If her husband and an innocent old woman weren't trapped inside, the sight would have been strangely beautiful.

Think.

It would take time for the flames to spread to the cabin. She had to douse them now.

How?

She had nothing to use to haul water from the stream. And the fire was spreading rapidly.

She searched the ground for a long stick, something she could use to pull back the ring of debris, create a pocket of space between the fire and the structure. She saw nothing.

But as she focused on the cold earth underfoot, a small, brown shape zigzagged past her in a blur, racing away from the back of the cabin toward the water.

She raised her eyes and let her gaze travel up the hill.

A second animal was darting down the hill behind the first. Strong thumping legs, long ears, fluffy, unmistakable bunny tail.

Her heartbeat ticked up, and she combed her memory as she followed its trajectory down to the water.

The Eastern cottontail rabbit didn't make its own burrows. It spent the winter holing up in tunnels dug by groundhogs and other burrowing hibernators. *Or by man.*

She spun back toward the cabin.

A stream of field mice and chipmunks were fleeing the fire behind the rabbits.

She sprinted toward the back of the structure. The kindling was fully engulfed now and the flames were roaring. A wall of heat hit her in the face. She stared hard at the ground, searching desperately for a way in that wasn't cut off by the fire.

And then she saw it. A terrified vole burst out from beneath the far right corner of the structure and dodged the circle of flames.

She dropped to her belly and crawled along the hard ground on her elbows, shivering in her cold, wet clothes. When she was five or six feet short of the house, she started digging furiously.

She scooped the hard earth and threw it wildly over her shoulder for a few moments. Then she stopped and lay there panting. This would take forever.

Think like a tunnel dweller.

Some of the animals were coming above ground, but most of them probably followed their tunnels to a ravine near the stream. She ran back to the water and squatted along its edge.

She didn't have to wait long before a large groundhog popped up from the stream and darted into the trees.

She ran to the spot where it had appeared and there it was: her way in. The mouth of a tunnel was dug into the bank. It was covered by the bare limbs of an overgrown tree. During the spring and summer months, it would be nearly undetectable behind its curtain of foliage. But she could see it clearly behind the skeletal winter limbs.

She waded to the opening and then plunged into the dark earth.

The tunnel was larger than she'd expected, smooth-walled and cold. She jogged forward, stumbling over rocks and fleeing rodents.

She reached for her flashlight, but her pocket was empty. She'd probably lost it when she dove into the stream.

She pressed on as quickly as she could in the dark, close space. The thin light that had filled the tunnel's mouth dissipated into blackness. She couldn't see her hand in front of her face.

Use your fingers then. Use your ears. And your toes.

Six-year-old Aroostine could track a deer through a thicket while blindfolded. Grown-up Aroostine could surely feel her way through a cave.

The ground rose under her feet as she worked her way uphill. The pungent smell of fresh dirt filled her nose. The sound of the skittering rodents gave her comfort. She couldn't hear or smell, or feel the warmth of the fire. So at least she knew she wasn't walking blindly into an inferno.

After several long minutes, the tunnel widened, and the ground beneath leveled into a cave.

She reached out and touched the side of a wall. She ran her hand along the wall and stepped slowly, waiting to kick an old potato bin or canning jar, proof that she was in a cold cellar.

For several agonizing seconds, she felt nothing but bare rock under her fingers and smooth earth under her feet.

Then her hand connected with a dowel of splintered wood. She reached above and felt another. Then another. Rungs to a ladder.

She gripped the sides of the ladder and hoisted herself up, feeling for the bottom rung with her foot. She slipped once, her hands sliding down the sides of the ladder and her chin butting against the cold, bare wall of dirt.

She steadied herself and continued to scrabble upward until her head bumped up against something solid. She ignored the stinging pain and reached up with one hand to touch more wood.

If she was right, she was under the floor of the cabin. And if some long-dead cabin dweller had dug out a cellar for vegetables or cold storage and gone to the effort of putting in a ladder, there had to be a trapdoor that opened into the house somewhere.

She clung to the ladder one-handed and ran her other hand along the wood overhead, searching for a hinge, a latch, something.

She felt nothing.

There *had* to be a way in. She stopped and inhaled slowly. *Calm down, slow down, and you'll find it,* she promised herself.

She started again, moving her free hand slowly across the wood. Her right arm, wrapped around the ladder's rail, began to ache.

She felt nothing to indicate there was a door leading into the cabin.

Maybe the wood had been replaced and the trapdoor removed?

Surely by now the fire department should have arrived, anyway. *If* Franklin had heard her message and called them.

Competing thoughts, hopeful and defeated, swirled through her brain. She'd gotten so close. She'd thrown the trial. She'd let the man escape, focusing instead on reaching Joe and Mrs. Chang, and for what?

She was hanging from a ladder, unable to help Joe and Mrs. Chang, who were just feet above her.

She pounded the wood overhead in frustration.

Thud.

The sound echoed through the cellar.

She made a fist and knocked against the wood again. And again.

Thud. Thud.

Her fist ached. She stopped to listen, but heard no movement above.

She punched again, harder.

Thud.

Dirt shook loose from the wall.

Tears stung her eyes.

As she pulled her sore hand back, ready to strike again, the floor above her head creaked and light flooded the dark space, momentarily blinding her.

She blinked up to see Joe and an old Asian woman with rags covering their noses and mouths. They stared down at her wide-eyed.

Behind them, the small room was hazy with smoke.

"Come on!" Joe urged her.

She extended her hand, and Joe gripped it. His hand was warm and callused. Just like she remembered. He hoisted her up through the trapdoor.

"You must be Aroostine," Mrs. Chang noted, her tone polite and friendly, given the circumstances.

"I am. I'd love to chat, but don't you think we should get out of here?"

Joe stared at her, his mouth slightly agape. She was sure she looked like someone who'd spent the night sleeping on the ground, been doused with gasoline, and then stumbled through a dark cave. But she couldn't exactly find it in herself to be embarrassed by her appearance.

What was *with* these two?

"Are you in shock?" she asked Joe carefully. Did shock victims even know they were in shock?

A slow smile broke across Joe's face.

"I think we're a little stunned, is all. How'd you get in?"

"There's a cellar dug out beneath the cabin. A tunnel leads from the cellar down to the stream. Let's go, already."

She looked around the smoky room.

Mrs. Chang followed her gaze. "The cabin's not on fire. Yet. Joe says these old logs will withstand a lot. I mean, don't misunderstand, I'm not interested in becoming human barbecue, but we don't seem to be in imminent danger." She smiled sleepily.

Aroostine wasn't sure she agreed with that assessment. Their weird behavior triggered a memory, and her mind flashed back to a time when her biological parents had still been alive.

She must have been five or six. Her parents had been out partying and had driven their old car into her grandfather's barn to keep it out of an impending rainstorm. After her father had parked, he'd passed out with the engine still running. Her mother had stumbled into the house and crashed on the couch.

When her grandfather found her dad still in the car, he was already suffering from carbon monoxide poisoning. She could see herself, standing barefoot in the rain in her green and pink nightgown, watching her grandfather try to coax and carry her uncooperative, dazed father out of the barn. She ended up dragging one arm, and they managed to move him to the house.

"Smoke and carbon monoxide are smart predators," her grandfather later explained. "They lull you to sleep and wait until you're defenseless to attack."

She swallowed around a lump in her throat and spoke in a calm, measured voice.

"We need to go. I'll help Mrs. Chang down the ladder and come back for you." She stared hard at Joe to make sure he was listening.

After a moment, he nodded slowly.

"Okay. Stay right there."

"Roo—" he began in a slurred, affectionate voice.

"Not now, Joe. We can talk later."

She turned and looped one of Mrs. Chang's arms around her shoulder. Then she walked the woman to the edge of the trapdoor and considered her options.

"Okay, I'm going to climb down first. Then I need you to take my hand, okay?"

Mrs. Chang grinned lazily.

This wasn't going to work.

"New plan."

Aroostine lifted the frail old woman over her shoulder and turned and backed into the trapdoor. Mrs. Chang hung limp and nearly weightless. Her arms dangled over Aroostine's back as Aroostine carefully worked her way down the ladder.

Mrs. Chang's feet bumped against Aroostine's knees in a rhythmic motion with each step Aroostine took.

After what seemed like days, she reached the cellar floor. She let Mrs. Chang slide to the floor and rested her against the wall.

"I'm going to go get Joe now," she explained.

The woman mumbled something unintelligible.

Aroostine climbed back up the ladder, much faster than her first trip now that the light from the cabin filtered down to guide her.

She pulled herself up into the kitchen and looked around. No Joe.

Un-freaking-believable.

"Joe?" she called.

Her voice echoed in the empty room.

She pressed her sleeve over her mouth and nose and hurried across the kitchen to the adjoining room. Inside, two thin mats were pushed to one corner. Joe stood in front of the small square window with a sock in his hand. The glass was smashed out.

Smoke poured through the broken window.

"Joe? What are you doing?"

He dropped the sock to the floor with a thud and turned toward her voice. His eyes were glassy and unfocused.

"Gotta get out . . ."

He gestured toward the window.

"That's not the way out. Come on, come with me."

He ignored her and shoved both arms through the opening, as if he were doing the breaststroke.

She screamed and raced across the room to tug on his shirt.

"Joe, you're too big, and the cabin's surrounded by fire!" She pulled him back into the room, praying he wouldn't slice an artery on the jagged shards of glass framing the window.

"You're on fire!" she shouted in horror.

He jerked his head to the side and saw the flames licking at his shoulder. He threw himself to the floor and rolled from side to side.

Her sweatshirt was still damp. She stripped it off and balled it up.

"Here." She crouched beside him and pressed the damp cloth against his smoldering shoulder.

"Thanks."

She searched his eyes. The pain seemed to have cleared his mind. He looked focused, alert. "Can you get up and follow me?"

He nodded.

"Okay, let's go."

She led him through the smoke-filled structure and to the trap-door.

"Can you manage?"

"Yeah."

He coughed before descending the ladder. She followed behind, going slowly, so she wouldn't bump into him. Now that they were out of immediate danger, her heart overtook her brain, and a wave of sadness and hurt washed over her.

Below her, Joe dropped to the ground and joined Mrs. Chang near the wall.

Aroostine clattered down the remaining rungs.

Mrs. Chang pulled herself up to a standing position.

"Okay, let's do this in a chain," Aroostine said.

She took Mrs. Chang's left hand and waited until Joe reached for the woman's right hand. Then she led them along the tunnel down toward the ravine.

She shuffled along, forcing herself to move slowly even though she wanted to run to the opening. They took small, uneven steps. Mrs. Chang stumbled, and Aroostine slowed her pace even more.

Her lungs screamed for fresh, cold air.

Behind her, Joe was coughing.

Finally, she heard the water below and pulled them forward toward the sound.

Her chest burned with every breath she took.

She tumbled out of the tunnel, and Mrs. Chang's hand slipped out of hers.

Aroostine collapsed on her back in wet, marshy grass. She could hear someone splashing through the water.

The light gray sky turned black.

CHAPTER FORTY-FIVE

Aroostine woke in a panic. Something was covering her face.

"Shh, shh. Take it easy," soothed a female emergency medical technician. "It's an oxygen mask. Don't touch. Anyway, you'll rip out your IV."

IV?

She turned her head to the side. Sure enough, an intravenous line was running from the back of her hand to a pole beside her. She let her eyes travel around the white, square space. She was in the back of an ambulance.

"Just fluids," the EMT chirped. "You're gonna be fine. Your friend's got a burn, but you don't have a mark on you."

Joe.

She tried to struggle to her elbows, but the EMT pressed her back with a firm hand.

"Listen, honey, it wasn't a bad one at all. They'll fix him up in no time. He's in the ambulance ahead of us with the old lady. You can see them after we get everyone checked out. You might as well relax. It's another twenty minutes to the hospital, even with Anthony driving this thing like he's in a NASCAR event."

Aroostine let her eyelids flutter closed and played back what she could remember.

The cave. The tunnel. The cellar.

She opened her eyes again and stared at the EMT, who was fussing with the bag of fluids.

She must have felt Aroostine's gaze on her because she looked over almost at once. Aroostine drilled her gaze into the woman's bright blue eyes and refused to blink.

The EMT sighed loudly, but her face softened with sympathy or something like it.

"All right, sister, you want me to tell you what I know?"

Aroostine nodded encouragingly.

The woman lowered herself onto what appeared to be an overturned milk crate.

"My name's Aimee, by the way. You must be Aroostine Higgins, because you don't look like you could be that Franklin dude's mother."

Aroostine widened her eyes at the mention of Franklin's name to let Aimee know she wanted to hear more. Was he here? Had she talked to him? Had they caught the man?

Aimee seemed to understand.

"He called 9-1-1 and reported an incident. Dispatch played the tape for us because it was kind of weird. He said the 'incident' was at an old log cabin made of aged white oak that sat up on a hill near a stream. Like, that's not how you report an emergency, you know? You give an address or a precise location. And, you know, you say there's a fire or a domestic dispute or whatever the incident is."

Aroostine bobbed her head so enthusiastically that the oxygen mask started to slip.

Aimee knitted her brows and frowned.

"Now, no more of that, or I'm not talking to you anymore," she chided as she readjusted the mask over Aroostine's nose.

Aroostine gave a very small, careful nod of understanding.

Aimee smiled and went on. "Anyway, it was clear he didn't actually know where the cabin he was describing was, if that makes any sense. He told the operator that his mother and an unrelated male were being held hostage in this cabin. Then, shortly afterward, he called back and said that some lawyer—I'm guessing that'd be you—went up to bust them out and found the place on fire."

She gave another tiny nod to confirm that Aimee had gotten the story right so far, or at least close enough.

"Lucky for you all, we knew exactly where the cabin was."

Aroostine tilted her head as if to say, *You did?*

"Yeah, sure. It's famous around here because it's the oldest standing structure in the county. Everybody knows the White House. We'd heard that some big-shot millionaire had bought it to restore it and turn it into a museum, but, as far as we knew, it was sitting empty."

She wondered whether the structure could be saved.

Again, Aimee seemed to read her mind.

"I think it'll have to be demolished now, but you never know. The firefighters were a good ten minutes behind us. When we got there, we called for a volunteer department over in Bridgeton to come out and lend a hand, too."

She fell silent for a moment.

Then she continued "You're all darned lucky your friend Franklin called us when he did. He reported that the suspect fled in a black Mercedes sedan. You don't see too many of them out this way, so Chief McClain set up road blocks at each entrance to the forest. He came out the west end and tried to drive right through the blockade. Last I heard, he's sitting in a cell with a sprained wrist. His head is pretty banged up, too, but from what I understand that happened at the cabin." She gave Aroostine a curious look.

Aroostine's heart was racing. They'd caught the man. They had to hold him until she could get in touch with Sid and let someone at Justice know.

It couldn't wait until she got checked out. The man could have unlimited reach. He'd make bail and disappear forever unless the federal agencies got involved.

She clawed the mask off and sucked in a harsh breath. "I need to call my office. It's urgent," she rasped.

Aimee gave her the stinkeye and slapped the mask back over her mouth.

"No way."

Aroostine began to thrash. She'd tear out the intravenous line if that's what it took to get this idiot woman to pay attention.

"Oh, knock it off. Is your office down in DC? The feds?"

She nodded vigorously.

"Well, someone named Mitchell is already waiting for you at the hospital. Don't ask me how he got there so fast. I guess he's a better driver than Anthony. And the rest of your jackbooted thugs are swarming all over the property already."

Aroostine collapsed against the metal stretcher, limp with relief.

Mitch wouldn't let the man get away.

Joe and Mrs. Chang were going to be okay.

She closed her eyes and allowed herself to drift to sleep.

The beaver was waiting for her.

When it saw her, it rose on its hind legs. Its black nose quivered in the air.

She walked up to it and held out her hand.

The beaver nosed her palm. The wet, cold touch tickled her skin.

Then it turned its silver eyes on her and stared into her eyes for a long time, impassive and unmoving.

She couldn't look away.

The wind seemed to whisper her name in her grandfather's voice.

The beaver twitched as if it heard it too, then it slipped into the stream and silently swam away.

CHAPTER FORTY-SIX

Friday night

She woke again in a bright, white hospital room. A heavily starched sheet and thin blanket were tucked tightly around her body. She turned her head to the right. A metal stand holding a bag of fluids stood sentry over her, the liquid slowly snaking its way through the tubing and into her arm.

She turned her head the other way. A blue-cushioned chair was pushed against the wall near a window. Mitchell sat in the chair, staring at her. He looked tired. And worried.

She let her gaze drift to the window over his head. Through the slatted blinds, she could see dark slices of sky.

"You're awake. Do you want me to call a nurse?" he asked in a hoarse voice.

She shook her head. "No. What time is it?"

He checked his watch. "Almost eight thirty."

"Friday night, right?" She was pretty sure, but it didn't hurt to confirm it.

He gave her a small smile.

"Right. You've been here since early afternoon."

"How long have you been sitting there?"

"Since early afternoon."

His gentle eyes met hers and held her gaze. "You drifted in and out of sleep. I didn't want to leave in case you woke up."

A lump rose in her throat. And then she remembered. "Joe and Mrs. Chang. Are they—?"

"They're both going to be fine. He . . . Your husband . . . has a burn on his shoulder, but it'll heal fine. The doctors want to keep Mrs. Chang for observation. She inhaled a lot of smoke, and her condition was probably a little bit iffy in the first place, after being held captive for a week and a half. They set her broken fingers and tried to feed her some soup." He grinned.

"Tried to?"

"Apparently that's all she had to eat the entire time she was in the cabin. She sent her son out to find her a cheesesteak. And a beer."

Aroostine laughed a scratchy, dry laugh.

"They checked you out pretty thoroughly, too. Although, I think they had you sedated for a while because you kept pulling off the oxygen mask. You're lucky you didn't suffer more from smoke inhalation."

Her laugh faded, and her throat hurt. "I know."

"How'd you know about the Underground Railroad?"

"The what?"

"According to the locals, that cabin was once owned by an avowed abolitionist. It's been rumored for years that it was a stop on the Underground Railroad, but no one ever found that tunnel system. You just stumbled on it?"

"Oh. The tunnel . . . Rabbits." She didn't have the energy to explain in greater detail.

He fixed her with a look.

"It's a long story. What happened at court?"

"I told Rosie what you wanted her to do, so she didn't go to court. Judge Hernandez is apparently a big fan of the ten-minute rule. At 9:40 exactly, he declared a mistrial because no one from

Justice had appeared. He didn't have his deputy call over or anything—just issued the order. It showed up on the docket a few minutes later, and Sid went ballistic."

"But he had to know it was just Judge Hernandez being petty. He can refile—"

"I don't think it even bothered Rosie. She was too worried about you. She knew you wouldn't just blow off court, even if you were deathly ill. She was hounding me to tell her what was really going on. While I was trying to put her off, your boy Franklin called and told me you found the place where the guy stashed his mom and your husband. He said to hold tight and he'd be back in touch."

She smiled. Franklin had come through.

Mitchell continued, "But since I didn't actually have anything concrete to tell Rosie all morning, I just kept saying you were really sick. Finally, she'd had enough and said she was calling the Metropolitan Police and the FBI to report an officer of the court was missing. I begged her not to and told her to just keep working on tracking down the venture capital group. And, what do you know, she found your guy."

"She *did?*"

He nodded. "She did. Adan Tereshchenko."

"That's him? The investor?"

"Nope. The venture capital group was nothing more than a shell. She tracked down the 'lawyer' who met with Franklin. That guy was a hired actor, by the way, but he gave her *his* contact, who gave up Tereshchenko."

"She did all that today?"

"She said she had to do something to keep herself busy. She's really concerned about you."

"So, who's Tereshchenko?"

"We're still tying it down, but it looks like he's tied to Eastern European organized crime."

"Like, mobsters?"

"Something like that."

"Why?"

"Why were they so interested in your case, you mean?"

She nodded her head.

"It was the reference to the Ukrainian ballbuster on the tapes. This outfit used the venture capital group as a front to get in with SystemSource. Can you imagine how much power they might have had? The RemoteControl system has been sold to the governments of eleven countries. Just in the US, it controls the US Mint, our offices, large chunks of the financial systems—including the NAS-DAQ. For crying out loud, it controls the operating rooms at Walter Reed and the kitchen in the White House."

"It does?"

"Yeah, think about that for a minute. It could have been an absolute disaster, but they couldn't get in through Franklin's backdoor."

She smiled. "Really?"

"Really. Apparently four different hackers accepted a challenge posted on Silk Road to break in. Each of the four failed. And all four were unceremoniously shot point-blank for failing. The whole mistrial was just supposed to cause a delay long enough for them to figure out a way in."

Her smile vanished. She was suddenly cold. She tried to pull the blanket more tightly around her even though she knew the chill was coming from within.

"If he's willing to kill, why didn't he just kill Womback and Sheely?"

He cocked his head. "What do you mean?"

"If he didn't want the tapes to get out, wouldn't the surefire way to prevent it be to kill the defendants? No defendants, no trial."

"You're frightening, you know that?"

She blinked up at him and waited for him to go on.

"That was plan A, as it happens. He posted a job on Silk Road looking for an assassin. The CIA heard the chatter and had the marshals scoop up Womback and Sheely and their families weeks ago."

"They've been in protective custody this whole time?"

"Yeah, and Sid was not happy that nobody bothered to tell him."

She could only imagine. There was no turf war like an interagency turf war.

"Okay, he couldn't get to the defendants. Then why didn't he kill me outright? Or keep Mrs. Chang indefinitely and just have Franklin do whatever he needed done going forward?" The questions chilled her, but she had to know the answers.

"He's not really a street thug. He's in middle management or its criminal enterprise equivalent. He just wanted a way into the system. He didn't want to get his hands any dirtier than he had to, and he's smart enough to know subcontracting wet work is an excellent way to get dimed out as part of a bigger deal somewhere."

"No honor among thieves," she muttered.

"Exactly. He knew he could exploit Franklin, so he decided to handle it himself. But he also couldn't hold Mrs. Chang prisoner forever. He just needed a temporary fix. You should be glad he didn't post another job on Silk Road."

"You keep talking about Silk Road. I assume it's not a reference to the Chinese trade routes from the Han Dynasty."

He shook his head. "Where've you been? It's an Internet black market. We keep shutting it down; it keeps popping up again. Mainly it's a place to buy and sell drugs, but a little murder-for-hire or prostitution isn't unheard of."

Prostitution. She wondered fleetingly exactly how Tereshchenko had gotten to Joe at the bar. She pushed it from her mind

"Rosie figured this all out?"

"Some of it. But the rest is coming straight from the horse's mouth. The local cops around here are no joke. They had blockades set up faster than even we could have done it. They nabbed Tereshchenko coming out of the forest. He's in custody and *very* interested in cutting a deal."

"He's talking? Won't his bosses kill him?"

"Probably, but he's a dead man either way. He's facing a list of charges in Ukraine. If we extradite him, he'll be killed before he's out of the airport, and he knows it."

"So we got him."

"You got him."

"Um . . . Does that mean Sid's not mad anymore?"

Mitchell bit his lip. Then he said, "He'll calm down, but he's not going to let it go, Aroostine. You failed to appear in court. He's already placed you on unpaid leave for conduct unbecoming an attorney."

"Conduct unbecoming? No exception for extenuating circumstances?" She blinked up at him. Was he joking?

He looked away. "Yeah. I'm sorry."

She closed her eyes and tried to focus on all the good news. Joe was alive. Mrs. Chang was alive. *She* was alive. A truly evil man was in custody. But the news of her suspension still stung.

"Aroostine?" he asked in a gentle voice.

She opened her eyes. "Yeah?"

"For what it's worth, I think you did the right thing."

He moved closer to the bed and lifted her hand from the sheet.

His hand was warm on hers and his eyes bored into hers with an intensity that made her heart race.

"That's worth a lot."

He rubbed her palm with his thumb.

Her breath hitched in her throat.

"I'm glad," he said, leaning close.

She breathed in, gathering herself, and then exhaled slowly. She kept her voice soft. "I love my husband."

Pain flashed in his eyes, but he didn't release her hand. "I know."

"Okay." She looked pointedly at his hand.

"You still need friends, though," he said in a careful voice.

He smiled down at her, and she grinned back at him.

"That's true."

Then she felt someone watching her from the hallway. Her door was propped open, and Joe stood on the other side, dressed in his smoke-blackened street clothes. A bandage peeked out through his shirt collar.

They locked eyes for a long moment, and then he turned wordlessly and walked away.

"Uh-oh," Mitchell said, following her gaze and dropping her hand. "I'll go talk to him."

She shook her head. "Don't. It's okay."

She might still be in love with Joe, but he'd made his feelings clear when he filed for divorce.

"Are you sure?"

"Positive."

He frowned at that, but after a few seconds, he settled back into his chair. She leaned her head back against the hard pillow. She'd worry about Joe later.

CHAPTER FORTY-SEVEN

Two days later

Aroostine pedaled her bike along the trail to Mt. Vernon. She locked it up and hiked to the rock overlooking the Potomac River in the predawn light and settled in with her thermos of tea to await the sunrise and a new day.

She didn't know exactly how long she'd been sitting there when the shadow fell across her rock.

After all, she wasn't there to keep track of time. She was there to track the flight path of the birds overhead, the way a blade of dry grass wavered in the wind, the telltale gravel disturbance that a rabbit left behind when it ran through the brush.

She shielded her eyes against the sun that had climbed high in the cloudless sky and turned toward the shadow, expecting to see a park ranger wanting to make sure she was all right, or maybe a hiker in need of directions.

It was Joe.

And time, which had expanded and slowed its pace while she'd sat there, suddenly increased its tempo to keep up with her racing heart.

She found her voice and said, "How did you find me?"

Joe smiled the knowing half grin of a husband who knew every inch of his wife's body and every corner of her soul.

"Piece of cake. When you came out here over the summer to interview for the job, we hiked up here the morning before we left. Don't you remember?"

She didn't, actually. The long weekend they'd spent together— the first and last time Joe'd spent any time in the city with her— seemed like a lifetime ago. And, if she was being honest, she'd stuffed the memory out of mind because it was too painful to address.

But now that he was standing there, two feet away, it came rushing back. Their hand-in-hand walk along the National Mall, stopping to ride the carousel with all the sun-kissed toddlers, dinner at a tiny noodle shop where the steaming bowls of pho were both fragrant and filling and the tables were so close together that her legs brushed up against the woman sitting at the next table when she stood up to leave.

And the picnic. The simple lunch they'd shared on a boulder very much like this one, followed by the surprise that Joe had produced from the picnic basket—a bottle of champagne and two plastic flutes. He'd toasted her future—*their* future—in halting, heartfelt words that had left her giddy and flushed with excitement at the new chapter in their life together.

She blinked back the tears that threatened to overflow from behind her eyes.

"I haven't been back here since then. What made you think I'd be here now?"

He searched her face.

"I knew you'd need to find a quiet place to think. A place where you could see the sky and the water. I followed a hunch."

She managed a tremulous smile. "Good tracker instincts."

He grinned back. "I learned from the best."

They looked at one another for a moment, and she let herself enjoy the warmth of their banter.

Then she tilted her head and said, "I thought you left town."

He averted his gaze, looked out over the water, and said, "I was going to. I saw you with . . ."—he paused and tripped over the name but managed to get it out—"Mitchell in the hospital. You were holding his hand."

Aroostine's heightened emotions went flat. She was suddenly deflated, tired. "He's a friend. A friend who helped me save your life, don't forget. And if you have to know, I was telling him that I still love you."

Her pride was screaming at her for making that confession, but she ignored it. She wasn't going to let her desire for dignity blot out the truth. Joe wanted to make a life without her? Fine, she couldn't prevent that. But she could make sure he made his choices with complete knowledge of what he was leaving behind.

She raised her chin and met his gaze levelly and unblinkingly.

His eyes reflected the pain she felt.

"I know that now, Roo. Your bossy friend, Rosie, read me the riot act." He reached out and stroked her hair. "I love you, too."

Her breath caught in her chest and, for a moment, hope fluttered in her belly. Then she remembered.

"Right. So much that you filed for divorce."

"That's not fair."

"Really?"

He sighed. "Really. We had a good thing going. We built a life. You were the county's most-respected lawyer. My business was good. We had Rufus, the house, our friends. Weekends out at the lake. Skiing in the winter. Fishing in the summer. But that wasn't enough for you."

She opened her mouth to protest, but he kept talking. "I tried, I really tried to support what you want. But I can't."

Tears stung her eyes. "I just want to *do* some good, Joe. You know, make a difference. Change the world. Don't you have those big, secret dreams?"

He smiled at her, a crooked, sad kind of smile.

"No, Warrior Girl. I don't. My dreams are pretty humble, and they aren't exactly a secret. Love my wife. Love my work. Maybe make a couple of little Jackmans to play with. Raise them right so maybe *they* can change the world. That was enough for me. That *is* enough for me."

He reached into his pocket. He pulled out a crumpled white envelope and pressed it into her hands.

She peeked inside. It was filled with gray ashes.

"What's this?"

"The divorce papers. I called my lawyer and told him to withdraw it. Then I burned my copy."

She stared down at the fine, burned particles for what felt like several hours and listened to her heart hammer in her chest.

"What does this mean, Joe?"

She looked up into his eyes. He held her gaze.

"What do you want it to mean?"

She wanted it to mean that her marriage wasn't dead, that they could start fresh, that the mess she'd made of her life wasn't permanent.

"I never wanted a divorce."

"I know, Roo." He dug his foot into the hard earth and kicked at a clump of clay with the toe of his boot. "Will you come home?"

He wanted her back. Her entire body went limp with relief. She saw herself curled into his side on the couch, snow falling soft and deep outside, Rufus trying to snuggle in between them, flames dancing in the fireplace.

But.

She'd be admitting she couldn't hack it at Justice. Proving Sid right. Could she really live with herself if she took off under a cloud of conduct unbecoming an attorney? Slinking out of town with Joe was tantamount to saying she didn't have what it took to be a federal prosecutor.

She'd worked too hard to concede defeat. *Hadn't she?*

Her relief dissolved into a puddle of dismay, and she felt utterly sick, like that time she wolfed down a corndog and then rode the Round Up at the county fair.

She remembered how Joe had held her hair back and rubbed her shoulders while she vomited into a rusty trash barrel conveniently positioned just outside the gate at the ride's exit.

He watched her now with sad, resigned eyes.

"You won't, will you?"

She closed her eyes and called up another image, this one of their wedding. A hot July Saturday. Bees hummed in the wildflower-dotted field behind their farmhouse. Her smooth cotton sundress, the daisies woven into her hair. His pressed slacks and the robin's egg blue shirt that made his eyes sparkle like the clearest ocean. They'd recited their vows full of hope, and love, and joy. It seemed so long ago and, at the same time, it could have been just last month.

The sun-kissed memory dissolved, replaced by a sharp, clear picture of the beaver.

It stood on its hind legs in a small stream. Long grass grew on the hilly bank, and an old elm shaded the water.

She knew that stream. It ran behind the barn where Joe had his workshop. She and Rufus loved to wade through it and look for frogs after she finished her work for the day and locked up the small office on the square.

Are you telling me to go home? She formed the question silently in her mind.

The beaver turned its silver eyes and stared at her wordlessly. A bird swooped low just above its head, and the wind carried it away over the hill. The beaver didn't move; its eyes were locked with hers.

"Aroostine?"

Joe's voice jolted her back to reality, away from the stream in Pennsylvania, to the craggy boulder in Virginia.

She'd spent most of her life distancing herself from her animal spirit guide and everything it meant. She'd ignored her nature to fit into the larger world. Was she now really going to let an imaginary beaver tell her what to do?

She looked at Joe for a moment before she slid down from the rock.

She stepped forward and slipped her hand into his.

"Let's go home," she whispered.

ACKNOWLEDGMENTS

My heartfelt thanks to the Thomas & Mercer team, especially Alison Dasho, Ben Grossblatt, Jamie Pierce, and Nicole Pomeroy, who were instrumental in bringing 'Roo to life. Special thanks also to my husband and children, who had to fend for themselves around my deadlines and who managed beautifully.

ABOUT THE AUTHOR

Photo © 2012 Frances Civello Photography

Melissa F. Miller is a *USA TODAY* Best-selling Author of more than a half-dozen novels, including the Sasha McCandless legal thriller series. She is also a commercial litigator. She and her husband now practice law together in their two-person firm in South Central Pennsylvania, where they live with their three young children, a lazy hound dog, and three overactive gerbils. When not in court or on the playground, Melissa writes crime fiction. Like many of her characters, she drinks entirely too much coffee; unlike any of her characters, she cannot kill you with her bare hands.